Dear Superman,

I know it's you. You can't fool me, no matter what. Mom says I hafta leave you alone. She says you're not real, but I know you are..

Your friend Willie

P.S. Can Superman have kids?

D1115947

Please address questions and book requests to: Harlequin Reader Service
U.S.: 3010 Walden Ave., P.O. Box 1325, Buffalo, NY 14269
CAN.: P.O. Box 609, Fort Erie, Ont. L2A 5X3

RHODE ISLAND

KRISTINE ROLOFSON

Somebody's Hero

Harlequin Books

TORONTO • NEW YORK • LONDON
AMSTERDAM • PARIS • SYDNEY • HAMBURG
STOCKHOLM • ATHENS • TOKYO • MILAN
MADRID • WARSAW • BUDAPEST • AUCKLAND

HARLEQUIN BOOKS
225 Duncan Mill Road, Don Mills,
Ontario, Canada M3B 3K9

ISBN 0-373-47189-0

SOMEBODY'S HERO

Copyright © 1990 by Kristine Rolofson

This edition published by arrangement with Harlequin Books S.A.

® and TM are trademarks of the publisher. Trademarks indicated with
® are registered in the United States Patent and Trademark Office, the
Canadian Trade Marks Office and in other countries.

Printed in U.S.A.

Dear Reader,

One summer morning many years ago I sold a set of bunk beds to one of the most handsome men in the world. He should have been a movie star, but he turned out to be the new neighbor, the man who had bought the white-steepled church down the street and was converting it to a home. I took his twenty dollars, tried not to stare and wondered what would happen if he really was a famous actor. Would he want anyone to know? No. He'd be tired of Hollywood and ready to settle down, of course. I knew that I could come up with the right heroine for him, as soon as the last customer left the yard sale and I could get my hands on pencil and paper.

People in my life have influenced the characters in this story. The Halloween party, the potluck suppers, the Thanksgiving football game, pumpkin shopping and spicy dumplings at the Chinese restaurant were—and still are—part of my life.

Things in "Pritchard's Corner" haven't changed much, except the handsome neighbor sold his new home and disappeared before *Somebody's Hero* was published.

And yard sales just haven't been the same.

Kristine Rolofson

With love to my parents, Don and Ottis Winslow.
They remain a constant source of inspiration
with a romance that still continues
after forty-five years.
Now *that's* what I call
a happy ending!

1

THE KID WAS BACK. Jake watched from his perch on the scaffolding as the child sneaked through the black-topped area that had once been a parking lot. When he disappeared behind a pile of rubble, Jake sighed. Where would the kid go next, and why wouldn't he play in his own yard?

The warm September breeze, directly from the Atlantic Ocean, whipped across the rocky pastures and past the former Pritchard's Corner Baptist Church. The view from the scaffolding attached to the steeple was incredible. A few lazy cows moved slowly through the fields; beyond, a generous strip of ocean trimmed the horizon. It was the kind of day the locals told Jake was "so clear, you could see Block Island." Jake admired the faint outline of land, then turned his attention back to the plastic sheeting in front of him. The crew had left half an hour ago, but Jake wanted to cover the holes left when the stained-glass windows had been removed. He had to sleep in this place and had grown tired of mosquitoes chewing him up.

Kerchunk. The last corner was stapled. He saw the flash of sneakered feet round the corner of the building. Jake reluctantly tucked the staple gun into his tool belt and climbed down the ladder. He hated to quit working so soon, but he'd had it with this little intruder. The last thing he needed in Rhode Island was a lawsuit if this kid got hurt. He hoped the guys hadn't taken all the beer. He'd like to pop a cold one, sit in the shade and feel satisfied with himself. If he could stop this kid from hanging around, he'd have one less problem. And a whole lot more peace of mind.

"Hey, kid!" Jake turned the corner behind the building. Piles of old lumber and hunks of drywall lay on the pavement, a disaster waiting to happen, but a good place to play hide-and-seek. Then Jake saw him, crouched behind the outside stairway the congregation had used to enter church each Sunday morning. Taking a few long strides, Jake trapped the boy in the corner. "Kid, you and I have to talk."

A little voice asked, "We do?"

Jake put his hands on his hips and nodded. "Yeah. Where do you live?"

"Across the street."

"The cemetery's across the street."

The boy looked as if he wanted to run. Jake stood firm until the child answered. "Next to the cemetery, across the stone wall."

"Okay, kid. Let's go." Jake held out his hand and the boy stood up, looking smaller and younger than Jake had first thought. "How old are you?"

"Six."

Jake put a gentle hand on the boy's shoulder, guided him across the parking area and down the driveway to the road. "What's your name?"

"Willie," he muttered.

"Mine's Jake," he said, although the boy hadn't asked.

"Yeah, sure."

"You think I'm lying?" Jake hid a smile as Willie stopped and carefully looked both ways before crossing the empty street. The boy might be a trespasser, but he was conscious of safety.

"Where're we goin'?"

Jake steered him down the street. "Guess."

"My house?"

"Yeah."

"Why?" The boy's brown eyes were wide now, as if it had just dawned on him that he might be in trouble.

Jake ignored the question. The answer was obvious, even to a six-year-old. "Is your mother home?"

"Uh-huh." He sighed. "But she's busy."

Too busy to keep her son under control, Jake decided. Jake paused at a tree-lined driveway. "This it?"

The boy nodded, and Jake heard soft cursing. He saw her then, standing on the smooth, green lawn in front of the large, yellow house. She held a hammer in one hand and a piece of wood in the other and looked aggravated. She was shorter than the tall, California actresses he was used to. Nothing special, Jake decided, noting the woman's tan legs and skimpy black top. Her heart-shaped face held high cheekbones tinged with peach, and piled on top of her head was a streaky mixture of chestnut and copper hair. She hadn't seen them yet, intent as she was upon her hammering. Jake guessed she was trying to drive the stake into the ground, but wasn't having much luck.

He felt the boy stiffen under his hand. "This her?"

Willie sighed again. "Uh-huh."

The woman didn't look old enough to be the boy's mother, especially in cutoff jeans and a bra that looked like the top half of a bathing suit. Jake took a minute to enjoy the scene and then mentally shook himself. This woman was responsible for the little troublemaker beside him. He had to get back to business. Jake tightened his grip on the boy's shoulder and marched him across the lawn.

Willie's mother looked up, turning surprised, hazel eyes toward Jake and Willie. Jake eyed the hammer, wondering if she'd use it as a weapon.

"Is he yours?" It was an unnecessary question, but he had to say something.

Leah Lang nodded. She wasn't crazy about the way the tall, well-built man was holding on to Willie's shoulder. "Please take your hand off my son."

"Sure," he said pleasantly.

Leah looked down at her child. He chewed his bottom lip, but there was an almost triumphant gleam in his dark eyes. And no fear— Leah wished he might be just a little bit nervous. It didn't take a college degree to guess the boy was in trouble. "Willie, what's all this about?"

"I was just lookin' at the church."

"Just looking?" the man repeated dryly.

Leah stared at him. His voice was deep, with no trace of an Eastern accent. She was sure she'd never seen him before. He was dressed in a white T-shirt and blue jeans, a worn, leather carpentry belt slung low on his hips. A dark blue baseball cap, with the words Kennedy Construction lettered in red, perched above his dark hair. Gray eyes, dark lashes and a model's bone structure. Incredibly handsome, and unfortunately he knew it. He'd look more at home in a three-piece suit instead of sawdust-covered jeans, Leah decided. "What's going on here?"

Jake's voice was cool. "Your son has been spying on me for days now. I've told him—for his own safety—to quit hanging around the church. There's too much there to hurt him."

So this is the Superman Willie keeps talking about. "You're absolutely right," Leah said. "William?"

He kicked a sneakered foot against the grass. "Yeah?"

"Do you have something to say?" Leah's voice was mild, but she hoped her son would get the message.

"I'm sorry," he muttered.

Leah doubted the sincerity of her child's words, but the man seemed satisfied.

"I'll give you a tour of the place when it's finished, son."

Willie looked up at his mother. "Can I go now?"

"Sure."

He ran across the yard, past the large, yellow house and into the door of a smaller, white, two-story house that faced the vegetable garden. Leah turned back to the man in front of her. He didn't look as if he was in any hurry to leave. "Sorry about that," she said. "He really isn't the kind of boy who gets into trouble."

He nodded, but she thought he could have looked more concerned. "All right." He lifted the baseball cap off his head and rearranged his thick, dark hair with one hand before resetting the cap on his head. The gesture was surprisingly male and Leah's stomach tightened. "But," he continued, "if the kid, Willie, gets hurt on anything on my property, you could sue the pants off me, lady."

"Leah Lang," she said, transferring the hammer to her left hand and offering her right.

"Jake," he answered, completing the handshake.

He was used to shaking hands with women, Leah realized. His hands weren't as rough as she expected a carpenter's to be. She glanced at his cap. "Jake Kennedy?"

His voice was gruff. "Yeah. Nice to meet you." Then he dropped her hand and looked down at the crooked stake. "Do you need help with that?"

Leah realized she'd forgotten what she was doing. Not a good sign, she thought. "No, thanks, I can—"

"No trouble," he said, ignoring her protests. He pulled a hammer from his belt and with several swift strokes settled the stake solidly into the earth. "There. You're all set now." He backed up a step.

"Uh, look. I told you Willie doesn't usually get into trouble, but—" She hesitated. She was going to sound like an idiot.

"But?"

"He thinks you're Superman. In disguise, of course."

"*What?*"

Jake looked horrified, as if she'd just told him Willie thought he was Jack the Ripper. She tried to hide a smile. "He thinks you're really Superman," she repeated, "and that you're hiding something."

Jake avoided the laughing eyes of Willie's mother by pretending to swat a fly. How could a six-year-old boy nail him so quickly? "In Pritchard's Corner, Rhode Island?"

She shrugged. "Strange, but true."

"Your kid needs help, lady." *And so do I.*

The laughter faded from her eyes, and she bristled. "He just has a highly developed imagination."

Jake went for the bluff. "He has a highly developed sense of snooping and he's driving me crazy."

Her chin came up. "He'll stop."

"He'd better." Jake hoped he sounded threatening and mean. The woman didn't seem intimidated, though.

"He will," she insisted.

"Fine." Jake took a step backward.

"I promise he won't bother you anymore."

Jake nodded and walked out of the yard and down the driveway. He couldn't believe what had just happened. Here he'd been worried someone would recognize him from one of the most popular nighttime TV soaps in history, and a little boy had nailed him for a twenty-six-week stint as Clark Kent in an ancient, low-budget television series. So what did that prove? Jake argued with himself as he crossed the street and headed home. If he stayed away from schools and playgrounds, he might just have the peace and quiet he needed.

Once inside the church, Jake popped the tab off a frosty can of beer. The basement was cool, a welcome change from outside. The gray and yellow linoleum tiles were obscured by dirt; Jake's scruffy work boots left marks in the dust when he walked over to the corner and sat down on the rented cot. He took a deep swallow of beer and surveyed the mess. He couldn't continue to camp out here much longer. The gutted upstairs was just the start of the slow rebuilding process. The electrician had promised to begin rewiring tomorrow, and a plumber's estimate was due any day. It was going to get a lot worse before it got better.

Jake finished the beer and decided to head to the fish 'n' chips place he'd discovered near East Matunuck Beach. He liked to order from the take-out window, then lean against the truck and smell the Atlantic Ocean while he ate. A few minutes later, Jake drove slowly past William's driveway. The kid was nowhere to be seen, but a large, shiny For Rent sign topped the stake Jake had helped Leah hammer into the ground. Jake pressed down on the gas pedal and sped out of Pritchard's Corner, but the sign stuck in his mind.

"WILLIAM, YOU'RE IN TROUBLE." Leah plopped ice cubes into a tall glass of tea and joined her son at the kitchen table.

"I didn't do anything."

"Let me explain trespassing to you," she said, running out of patience.

Willie shrugged. "He won't call the police. Jake's a nice guy."

Leah raised her eyebrows. "Mr. Kennedy, you mean?"

"The guys call him Jake."

Leah took a swallow of ice tea. "You're not one of the guys. You're a little kid, who should be staying away from a construction site." She watched her son, chin in hand, stare down at the oak table. "Right?"

He looked up at her and grinned. "He looks just like Superman."

"Will—"

"Really! On Channel 39 at six-thirty."

"C'mon, Willie. Give it a rest." Leah was pretty damn tired of hearing about Superman. She'd had enough, especially since she'd been confronted by an angry carpenter.

"You'll see, Mom. Watch the show with me."

"No, thanks." The last thing she wanted to do at six-thirty in the morning was to watch an old television show. "And you're not, either. You're cut off from that TV show until further notice."

He was outraged. "Mom!"

"Too bad, love, but you pushed me." She drank the rest of her tea while her son sat in silent defiance. Leah wondered if she should be more understanding, especially since she was going to become a therapist. She should probably listen to her son's problems, allow him to have his fantasies. Had Willie identified with Superman because he had no father to look up to? Still, the boy needed to learn that trespassing was illegal, buildings under renovation were dangerous, and respecting your neighbor's privacy was important. "You're grounded, too," she added.

He sighed. "But what if he is?"

"What if he is what?"

"What if he is Superman?"

"Oh, Willie, please," she moaned. But she had to smile at the child. Jake Kennedy did look like a good candidate for Superman—tall, dark, strong and handsome. The kid had a point.

Willie opened his mouth to say something, then stopped.

"Look," Leah tried. "Superman can leap tall buildings in a single bound, right?"

He nodded.

"If you see our new neighbor jump over the church steeple, you let me know. *Then* I'll believe you."

His face lit up. "Okay."

"But you're to stay here, in your own yard, until further notice." Leah pushed her chair back and stood up. "School starts tomorrow, anyway."

"He wears blue underwear."

"Who, Superman?" Leah set her empty glass in the sink and tried to remember if he wore red tights with blue underwear or blue tights with red underwear.

Willie shook his head. "No. Jake."

"How on earth do you know that?" Was she raising a Peeping Tom? What was going on here?

Willie acted disgusted. "He made a clothesline."

She leaned against the counter and crossed her arms in front of her chest. "Your spying days are over, pal."

"We hafta go to town to get a lunch box."

"Good idea," Leah agreed, letting him change the subject. She was getting a little tired of it herself. She had more important things to think about. Tomorrow was Willie's first day of school. Next week her classes at the university started.

"ISN'T IT A LITTLE EARLY in the day for champagne?"

Leah jumped, losing her grip on the plastic cork. She looked up to see Jake Kennedy standing a few feet away in the yard. She supposed it did look a little strange. "It's the first day of school," she said, as if that fact explained everything.

He came closer. "Yeah. I saw all the mothers and kids waiting for the bus."

Leah couldn't help staring. He was just as handsome in the morning as he had been yesterday afternoon. Even wearing jeans and an inexpensive denim shirt, he looked as if he should be a model. "Is there, um, something I can help you with?"

He smiled, but his charcoal eyes held little warmth. He handed her a set of binoculars. "I think these belong to your son."

Uh-oh. "Thanks." Embarrassed, Leah took them, and set them down on the step. "I have a feeling I'm not going to like this."

"Willie was using them last night, just before dark. At first he sat on the wall in front of the cemetery, then he came closer, to the slope behind the church. He forgot the binoculars when I chased him off. Isn't he a little young to have the run of the neighborhood?"

Leah's distress increased. "I thought he was feeding his chickens and doing his chores."

Jake shook his head. "This has got to stop."

"I'm sorry," Leah said. "It's this Superman thing. I grounded him yesterday, but I'll have another talk with him."

"A talk?" He lifted one eyebrow. "You think that will stop him?"

"I hope so." That, and a much-needed spanking.

"Excuse me, but what about his father?"

The question was out of line, but it didn't seem to bother him. Leah looked Jake right in the eye. "I don't think that's any of your business."

"Maybe not, but the kid needs discipline."

"*The kid* has everything he needs."

Jake smiled. "Including a mother who drinks first thing in the morning?"

Leah wanted to hit him with the bottle she still held in her hand but kept her tone civil. "I'm having a party. You're welcome to stay and meet the neighbors."

"No, thanks." He made a move to turn away from the step and gestured towards the big, yellow house. "Who do I talk to about renting the house?"

"That's already been rented to college students." When he looked puzzled, Leah added, "The small cottage behind mine is the one for rent."

"Do I talk to you about it?" He didn't look pleased.

She nodded.

"You're in charge?"

"I own them."

"Well, I can't keep camping out in the church. The electricity has been turned off and the plumbing will be pulled out tomorrow. How much is the rent?"

Leah hesitated, wishing for the hundredth time that Mr. Marcetti hadn't moved to Florida to live with his daughter, then named the price. "But I don't think it would be suitable."

"Why not?"

"It's just one bedroom and very small. I only rent the place to elderly men who like to garden."

He stared at her. "Is that a joke?"

She shook her head.

"It's a little late in the season to plant anything," he said slowly. "But I'll pay whatever you're asking, if you let me rent without a lease. I plan to move back into the church as soon as it's livable."

Leah thought that would take more months than either one of them could count but bit back the words. "I'm sorry, but could we talk about this another time? I'm having company."

He stepped closer and held out his hand. "Give it to me."

Leah realized he meant the champagne bottle. She handed it to him without a word and watched as he quickly popped the cork and sent it sailing into the air. She supposed he'd be happy now that he'd done his good deed for the day.

"I hate doing that," she said.

"I could tell by the way you were frowning at it when I walked up." He handed her the bottle. "Now, about the house—"

"Please—"

He ignored her. "At least Willie wouldn't have to leave the yard to spy on me. I assume there are curtains on the windows?"

"Yes, but—"

"Can I look at it?"

Leah gave up. He could look all he wanted to, but she didn't want to rent the place to a stranger like Jake Kennedy. "Go ahead," she said with a sigh. "It's unlocked."

"Thanks." He flashed her a charming grin. "I'm willing to pay the first and last month's rent, plus a damage deposit. I've never grown a vegetable in my life, but I don't give wild parties or throw garbage out the door."

Leah picked up the binoculars and opened the kitchen door. "Thanks," she said. "I'll keep that in mind."

2

"No!"

Leah turned off the television set over Willie's protests. "You're becoming a little television freak."

"It's cuz I'm grounded," the child muttered, slumping down on the overstuffed couch.

"Because you won't quit bothering Mr. Kennedy," she reminded him. The last couple of days had been quiet, but it was now Friday afternoon and Leah hoped Willie would remember Wednesday's long talk about respecting people's privacy.

Leah surveyed the living room. The plaster walls needed a fresh coat of white paint and the wood floors could use a thorough mopping, but housework wasn't her favorite thing to do. Her grandmother's braided rugs absorbed a lot of dust; their faded appearance gave them an antique look. The oak furniture, too, was simple and old, having been in the family for as long as anyone could remember. It was a good thing she'd inherited the furniture, Leah thought, because she could never have afforded to buy it. Her one splurge had been the lace curtains, on sale at Sears three years ago. Leah noticed Willie's name printed neatly in the dust on a bookshelf. She either had to get out of the house or clean it. "C'mon, Will, let's go see if the car is fixed."

He turned twinkling brown eyes on her. "I'm grounded."

Leah laughed. "I give you permission to leave the yard with me."

He jumped off the couch and hurried to follow her out the door. It was a short walk, less than half a mile along the quiet road. The gas station at the end of the street was Pritchard's Corner's only industry besides the farms and the state fish hatchery.

"Junk it," Steve said, shaking his head. He shoved a greasy rag into his back pocket and pointed toward the hood of the white car. "It needs a new engine, and you could buy a used car for what that would cost."

Leah's heart sank. She had depended on Gibson's Garage to fix her aging Cadillac more than once, especially lately, and she wasn't prepared for bad news. "But I just put new brakes in it six months ago."

He shrugged. "If I've learned one thing in this business, it's that there's no sense throwing good money after bad."

Leah tried to smile. "Thanks." The mechanic had always been honest with her. There was no reason to question his judgment, but the news hurt. "What do I do now?"

"I'll arrange to have it sold for parts if you want to leave it here," he offered. "I'll let you know if I hear about any decent cars for sale."

"It'll have to be cheap," Leah said, running her hand over the hood of her grandmother's old Cadillac. She'd inherited the car along with everything else five years ago. "When I was sixteen, my grandmother taught me how to drive in this car."

Steve nodded. "Yep, I've put a few million gallons of gas in it, I think."

He left to pump gas for a waiting customer, and Leah emptied the car's glove compartment while Willie checked under the seats for missing toys. Leah hated parting with the car. It had carried her mother back and forth to the doctor, brought her baby home from the hospital, and held her in luxurious comfort when she'd pulled over to the side of the road to cry, after she'd buried the two women she'd loved most in the world. Now the old Caddy's shabby interior often smelled of French fries and bubble gum, it didn't like to start in cold weather, and an embarrassing trail of smoke billowed out of the exhaust pipe.

"Now what, Mom?" Willie tugged at her blouse.

"We walk," she said, shoving the papers into her shoulder bag.

"Are we gonna get a new car?"

"Good question." Leah sighed. Her college classes started next week, and Pritchard's Corner wasn't exactly teeming with public transportation. Maybe she could hitch rides with the students next door until she bought another car. That is, until she figured out how she was going to afford to buy a car on this year's tight budget.

When they reached their driveway, Leah looked over toward the church. The white siding was being replaced by wood, and the constant hammering sounds meant Jake and his crew were taking advantage of every hour of daylight. She noticed a few new windows, but plastic still covered most of the holes. The old dame was having a face-lift, but the bandages were still on.

"He's here." Willie cheered.

Leah looked away from the building and down at her grinning child. "Who?"

"You know—Superman."

Leah stifled a groan. *Patience. He's only six.* "Don't start this again, William." She looked to where he pointed and saw Jake near the stone wall that separated her property from the graveyard. He walked toward them across the grass. "What do you think? Did he leap over the wall in a single bound?"

"Nah. It's not high enough."

"I was just kidding," she said as she waited in the driveway. "Maybe you should thank him for returning the binoculars."

Willie edged away. "You think he's still mad?"

"Have you been staying home?"

"Yeah," Willie called, running around to the back of the farmhouse.

The guilty look on Willie's face made Leah wonder. Was there going to be another confrontation about Willie's spying? She glanced at Jake. The man certainly had presence, she thought as she watched him stride toward her. He had a walk that commanded attention, an easy grace that caused Leah to suspect Jake was used to having people look at him. But why? She didn't understand it. Why would she think she'd seen him somewhere before? And how could she blame William for thinking this man was someone special?

As he came up to her he tipped his baseball cap. "Ms. Lang," he drawled. "How are you this afternoon?"

"Just fine, Mr. Kennedy," she lied. She really wanted to go into her house, fix a large, cold glass of iced tea and work on her budget. She didn't want to make polite conversation with the man across the street. "And yourself?"

"Not so good. That's what I wanted to talk to you about."

"All right."

"The offer to rent the cottage still stands." He put his hands on his hips. "I'm getting tired of sleeping in sawdust and breathing insulation. Your place would be pretty convenient, so I'll double my offer."

Double? Leah began to open her mouth, but he held up a hand.

"Don't say no right away. Think about it."

"But—"

"Just think about it. That's all I ask," he said and turned to go back to the church.

Leah didn't want to think about it. She should have said, *Okay, you can have it. Here's the key.* It didn't take a financial genius to realize that her carefully planned budget was shot to hell, and that the money for a new car had to come from somewhere. Jake had stood right in front of her, offering the light at the end of the tunnel.

And she didn't want to take it.

Leah walked up the gravel driveway and saw Willie hiding behind a tree. "You can come out now," she said. "He's gone back to work."

"Good." He frowned at his mother. "He probably saw me anyway."

"Why?"

"X-ray vision."

"You're only six years old. How do you come up with all this stuff?" But Willie didn't hear her, he was already running off to play. Leah went inside the quiet house and, ignoring the pile of papers stacked beside her computer, sat down at her desk. She fiddled with dollar figures and then gave up. The solution remained with the little rental cottage. The income from renting the large house paid the property taxes, living expenses and contributed to the savings account that paid her college tuition. Her typing business bought food and clothes. But the cottage income supplied the life insurance payment, so Willie would be provided for, should anything happen to his one and only parent.

Jake had offered to pay double what she was asking. The extra money would be the difference between wheels and walking. The only other person who'd stopped and asked her about renting the place was Paul, the fifteen-year-old who lived next door and was always trying to figure out how to get away from his parents. She had no choice but to accept Jake Kennedy's offer.

Later, after supper, she took Willie over to the church with her. "Don't touch anything," she warned as they approached the building. She gripped his little hand. "And don't get near any of this lumber."

Piles of splintered wood covered most of the parking lot. Except for a red pickup truck there was no sign of the crew. The place was silent.

"He lives down there," Willie said, pointing to the basement door.

"Well, you ought to know." She held his hand a little tighter and wove a careful path through the rubble to the church's basement entrance. They went down the steps and she knocked.

The wooden door opened to reveal Jake. The surprised look on his face made Leah want to smile. He wore a clean, white T-shirt and jeans and had a paper towel in his hand. "Hello."

"Hi." Leah could smell pizza. "Did we interrupt your dinner?"

He smiled and Leah felt her face warm. She also felt ridiculous. "Yes," he said, taking a step backward to let them enter, "but I don't mind at all. Come on in and I'll give you the tour I promised."

Leah stepped inside and was immediately overcome by guilt for hesitating to rent Jake the cottage. A rumpled sleeping bag lay on a simple cot in the corner of the church's large kitchen and dining area. The counters were littered with tools, papers and blueprints. A microwave oven sat amid the mess. Boxes were stacked from floor to ceiling against one wall.

"Excuse the mess," Jake said, tossing the paper towel

onto the counter. "But maybe you'll feel sorry for me and let me rent the cottage."

"It's yours."

He sighed. "Great. There's only so much of this I can take, and I think one month is enough."

"You've lived here a whole month?" It was worse than she'd thought.

"It wasn't this bad at first, believe me."

"I think it's neat," Willie said, bouncing on the cot. "Like camping."

"Well, I guess so." Jake waved his hand at a flat, white box on the counter. "Do you want some pizza? There are a few pieces left."

"Uh, no, thanks," Leah said. "But don't let us keep you."

"I'll eat some!" Willie jumped off the cot and looked into the box. "Can I pick the mushrooms off?"

"Go ahead," Jake said. "There's soda in the cooler over there. Help yourself while I give your mom a tour of this place. Just don't touch anything."

"Neat." Willie lifted the lid of the cooler and rummaged through the icy water before choosing a can.

Jake turned back to Leah. "Now, what about you?"

"I don't need anything, thanks."

He smiled, a slow charming smile that lighted up his eyes, and Leah wondered if he practiced in front of a mirror.

"Come on." He held out his hand. "I'll show you what I'm working on."

Leah had to admit she was curious. The whole town was. For months the sale of the church had been the talk of Gibson's nine o'clock coffee break and the object of speculation from those who took daily walks along Old Post Road. "You've caused a lot of curiosity around here, you know."

He looked pointedly at Willie. "I realize that."

"That's not exactly what I meant. The whole town is dying to see what you're doing with this place. It's quite a landmark."

"That's what attracted me in the first place." Jake gestured toward a doorway in the back of the room. "Come on, then. You'll be the first person in town to see the inside work. We can go upstairs this way."

Leah hesitated briefly. She didn't know anything about house remodeling, but it might be interesting to see how someone turned a church into a home. "All right," she agreed. Willie sat on the floor guzzling root beer and looked perfectly content. "Wait right here," she told him. "I'll be back in a minute."

"Okay."

She gave him a look that was intended to say *If you do anything to get into trouble, you'll be grounded for the rest of your life.*

"O-kay," he said again.

Leah followed Jake into the hall. "I think these other small rooms down here were for Sunday school classes," he said. "I'm going to make bedrooms out of them."

"Oh. Good idea." Leah thought it was awfully hard to tell what anything was going to look like, because there were so many areas that were just framed with wood.

"It's a mess," he continued. "I'm going to have to redo the wiring and the plumbing."

"You don't sound too concerned." The vast scale of the job impressed Leah, and she carefully walked between the framed doorways, avoiding piles of nails and sawdust on the cement floor.

He smiled. "That's part of the fun. And I'm not in any hurry, at least not now that I have another place to live."

"I thought time was money in the construction business." He didn't seem to lack either, she guessed, and followed him to a wide stairway where he politely waited for her to take the lead.

"It should be that way," his voice rumbled behind her. "But this project is a little different."

"Why is that?"

"Kennedy Construction was my father's business. I came into it recently when he died."

"I'm sorry," Leah said. *Who are you?* was what she really wanted to ask. The stairs curved and opened onto the main floor. Leah had been there once with her grandmother. The rows of oak pews and the stained-glass windows had been removed, probably transported to the new church a mile away. The room was enormous, even though it was filled with stacks of lumber and drywall.

"This will be the living room," Jake said. "I'm putting in a kitchen back there, with a large work counter. It will all be open."

"It's beautiful," Leah answered. The huge windows by the ceiling were covered with plastic, but even so light brightened the room. "I see why you don't want to break up this space."

"Come over here for a second." He put his hands on her shoulders and turned her around. "See up there?"

Leah looked up at the choir loft. She nodded, aware of the warmth of his large hands.

"Master bedroom. I may put in skylights, if I decide I need more light. Also a bathroom."

"There's room?"

"It's larger than it looks. I'd let you go up, but there's only a ladder now. We had to remove the old stairway."

Leah turned to face him. He was standing uncomfortably close to her. "Are you actually planning to live here?"

He grinned. "I know what you're thinking—it's a big place for one person, right?"

His eyes were the most intriguing combination of gray and silver. She nodded, forgetting what she had asked.

Jake shoved his hands into his pockets and looked around the room. "I may or may not live here, but this place interested me from the moment I saw it. And I needed a big project."

"You're not from around here, are you?"

"Upstate New York. Did you know that this property was advertised all over New England?"

Leah hadn't known, but she supposed it made sense. Not many local people could afford to tackle such a large renovation. She walked over to one new window. "You have a wonderful view, too."

"I can see the ocean, the cows and the cemetery." He stepped closer to her. "And your house. I'll be in great shape when I get more windows."

He was in great shape now. And that deep voice slipped over her spine like melting ice cream. *It's just hot in here,* she told herself. In the last few years, September had been an unseasonably warm month. "Well," she said, clearing her throat. "Thanks for the tour. I'd better be getting home." She edged toward the stairs.

"I'll grab some of my things and come with you."

"But the cottage isn't ready."

"It's empty, isn't it?"

"It's not clean. I have to do that before you move in."

"No, you don't. You've seen how I'm living now. Do you think it matters to me how the cottage looks?"

"It matters to me." His disgusted expression did nothing to detract from his good looks. Leah decided she could be just as stubborn as Jake Kennedy.

"Then when?"

Leah thought quickly. She still had the large house to finish cleaning tomorrow, before the girls arrived Sunday afternoon, and two financial statements to type for one of the neighbors. "Sunday."

He shook his head. "No good. That's two more days, and I'll have no electricity and no water after tomorrow." Jake brightened. "I'll help you clean it now."

"You can't. I have plans tonight." Leah glanced at her watch. She'd almost forgotten the potluck birthday party at the Pattersons' house.

"When?"

"At eight."

"That's in two hours. We have plenty of time."

He wasn't going to take no for an answer. She should let him rent the house dirty, but doing that went against everything her grandmother had taught her about cleanliness. "You win, but we'll have to hurry."

"Great!" Jake put his hand lightly between Leah's shoulder blades and guided her to the stairs. "Just tell me what you want me to do."

"How are you with a mop, Jake?"

"Terrific."

Leah doubted that. The man looked as if he'd never scrubbed a floor in his entire life. On the other hand, he was probably an expert at telling people what they wanted to hear. The thought bothered her.

They arrived in the kitchen in time to stop Willie from trying to crush an empty soda can with his bare hands.

"You'll cut yourself," Leah warned. "Put it down."

Jake laughed, then took the can from Willie and easily crushed it with one large hand.

"Wow!" the boy said.

Leah sighed. "It doesn't take a lot to impress a first-grader."

"It always worked with the girls in junior high school."

Jake tossed the can onto the floor and began to roll up his sleeping bag. "Do you have sheets at your place?"

"I don't usually supply bedding, but in your case I'll make an exception."

"Fine." He smiled at her. "Real civilization."

"It doesn't take much to make you happy."

His gray eyes warmed as his gaze lingered on her face. "I wouldn't say that."

The man was flirting with her, Leah realized. Time to exit. She turned away and grabbed Willie's hand. "Let's go."

"I'll meet you at the house in a few minutes," Jake added, "as soon as I throw a few things in a bag and lock up here. I don't want you to change your mind."

"I won't," she promised, already halfway out the door. She pulled Willie up the concrete steps and along the parking lot.

"Mom," he panted, "you won't believe what I found."

Leah stopped at the edge of the road and waited for a car to pass. "What do you mean, you *found*? Were you snooping again?"

"Nope. I just wanted to look around a little, you know?"

"William…"

"I found a locked trunk," he said proudly, ignoring his mother's warning.

"Lots of people have trunks, Willie. That's how they store their belongings. Sometimes they keep them in attics, like we do, remember?"

"But, Mom, this one said J. Kent."

"So?" Leah began to feel sorry she'd taught him to read last year. She tugged Willie across the street, wondering where she'd left the mop. Maybe it was still in the big house.

"Don't you get it?" Willie's voice grew higher. "K-E-N-T. *Clark Kent*. Superman."

"Lord, Willie, are you going to keep this up?"

He ignored the question. "Kennedy isn't Jake's real name. Maybe *Jake* isn't Jake's real name. The trunk said *Kent*."

"You're only six. Why can't you play with matchbox cars like other kids?"

"Too boring," he scoffed. "I'll tell Paul. He'll understand."

"Fine," she said. "You do that. He's babysitting tonight, so you two can have a big conversation about Superman and locked trunks and—" Leah put her hands on her hips and looked at her son. "How did you know the trunk was locked?"

The boy was suspiciously silent, his sneakers making circles in the gravel.

"William? Did you try to open it?"

"Nah," he muttered. "I just wanted to see if the lid worked."

"Same thing, buster." Leah cupped his chin with her hand, forcing him to look at her. "Don't you ever snoop around other people's things again. Do you understand?"

He tried to nod.

Leah dropped her hand and pointed toward the house. "Go inside and get the toilet brush out of the bathroom. Since you have so much curiosity, you can check out the inside of a toilet bowl."

"Aw, Mom—"

"Don't 'Aw, Mom' me. We both have to work around here, and you're assigned to the bathroom of the little cottage."

"Is Jake movin' in?"

"Yeah." Leah heard the awestruck tone in her son's voice

and wondered what she was getting herself into. "Your hero is going to live right next door."

Later, standing in front of a sparkling-clean mirror, Leah realized she wasn't going to have time to wash and dry her hair. It didn't look too bad, she decided. She could pin it up on top of her head and use a fancy barrette. Leah picked up the bottle of cleaner and the roll of paper towels and left the bathroom. Jake stood in front of the kitchen sink, squeezing dirty water out of a mop.

"I think that's the worst of it," she told him.

Jake turned around and smiled. He leaned the mop against the counter and wiped his hands on a rag. "I like this place."

"It's small," she said. "It used to be a blacksmith's shop in the early eighteen hundreds." Now it held an L-shaped living room and kitchen, plus a small bedroom. The tiny bath that popped out from behind the kitchen had been added on to the original rectangle twenty years ago.

"I like it." Jake grinned. "No sawdust."

"Not much furniture, either, but I guess you don't care."

"As long as there's a bed and a refrigerator, I'm happy."

Leah decided not to comment. She couldn't picture Jake's large frame on Mr. Marcetti's narrow single bed, but she banished the intriguing image from her mind as she headed for the front door. "Well, if you're all set, I'll take off."

"Wait, Leah." He reached into the back pocket of his jeans and pulled out a black checkbook. "I'll write you a check for the rent."

"Tomorrow will be soon enough. I really have to go. I'm being picked up in half an hour."

But Jake followed her to the door. "You have a date tonight?"

"Not really." Patsy Farrel was constantly trying to fix her

up with an assortment of single doctors from the local hospital. There was no telling whom her best friend would bring to Jenny's birthday party.

"Well, have a good time." He reached out to open the door for her. "I take it you're not married."

"That's right." Leah stepped into the fading sunlight. The ocean breeze cooled her skin as she turned to see Jake framed in the doorway.

"You sound happy about it." He smiled, flashing perfect white teeth.

The observation made her smile. "I like my life the way it is. You're not married either, right?"

He shrugged. "I'm one of those confirmed bachelor types."

"You'd better watch out, Jake. There are six college girls moving into the big house on Sunday."

"Thanks for the warning," he drawled, not looking very concerned. "But I outgrew my teenager phase years ago."

She could not—would not ask him what phase he was in now. His eyes danced, as if he were daring her to ask. As if he'd love to answer. She doubted his lack of interest in the college girls. They'd adore having him next door and go out of their way to show him. "Well, enjoy the cottage," she said lamely before turning to walk the few steps to her own front door.

"Leah?"

She stopped again. At this rate she wouldn't have time to shower. "What?"

"Why'd you change your mind about renting this place to me?"

Leah shrugged. "It's not important."

"C'mon, tell the truth." His voice was pure charm.

"I need the money for school."

"School?" he echoed.

"I'm going back to college next week." Leah couldn't keep the pride—or the nervousness—out of her voice. "See you tomorrow, Jake."

So, Jake mused, watching Leah hurry into her own house, she had a social life. Why was he surprised? She was an attractive woman, but Jake'd bet money there weren't a lot of men lining up to take on fatherhood to that weird kid of hers.

Jake firmly shut the door. He had come to Rhode Island to work, to concentrate on the real world, to escape from lust and power and stardom. But he'd just used his money and charm to maneuver a perfectly nice woman into renting her dwarf-sized house and he didn't feel the least bit guilty. Jake was disgusted with himself. The years in L.A. must have gone to his head.

3

THE HEAVY BEAT of Paul's favorite rock group hummed through the floorboards of Leah's attic bedroom. Leah, dressed in casual, beige slacks and a fashionably oversize copper jersey, flipped gold hoops into her earlobes.

Tonight would be fun. Her friends, most of whom were married, liked to give informal potluck parties where everyone mixed and mingled. It was rarely obvious or awkward to attend one of the parties as a single woman. The only bad part was driving home alone. The winding, country roads seemed awfully dark when she was driving by herself. Tonight she was lucky because Patsy and Joe would pick her up. She took one last look into the mirror before hurrying downstairs.

"Hi, Paul. I hope Willie doesn't understand the words to this song," Leah said to the teenage boy sprawled on the couch playing Go Fish with Willie. The lyrics blasted the joys of sex over the guitars and drums.

"Not many people do," Paul said. "Hey, you look hot."

"I know." Leah sighed, lifting her long hair off her neck. "It's still pretty warm upstairs."

"No." He laughed. "I meant you look *hot*, you know— like you look really nice."

"Gee thanks, Paul," Leah said. Compliments were rare from the teenager. "I appreciate that."

She looked helplessly around the living room. Willie had

taken his toys back to his bedroom, but the place still looked cluttered. "Anyone seen my sandals?"

"Under the desk," Willie yelled. "Can I watch a movie? Paul brought some tapes."

Leah turned down the volume of the stereo and retrieved her leather sandals. She looked guiltily at the computer. She could have spent all evening catching up on her typing if she hadn't been going out. But surely she deserved some time for fun, she told herself as she straightened the pile of papers and stuck loose pens into the colorful pencil holder Willie had made in kindergarten. "How's school going, Paul?"

"Spanish still suc—rots. It's okay, I guess." He looked over to Willie. "Do you have any threes?"

"Go fish. What about the movies, Mom?"

A car honked in the driveway, and Leah blew her son a kiss. "You can watch one of them, as long as you're in bed by ten and whatever one you pick won't give you night-mares."

"*Superman III*'s okay, isn't it?" Paul called.

"No." She groaned inwardly, thinking of Jake. "But Willie can watch it anyway." She grabbed a platter of deviled eggs from the refrigerator and headed out the door. "The phone number's by the telephone!"

The only answer was the higher volume of the music.

Jake strolled across the yard in time to see a car back up and turn around in the large driveway. Good. He'd timed it perfectly. He wanted to see what kind of man Leah Lang went out with. Just simple curiosity, he told himself.

Jake watched as Leah stepped outside and walked to the car. He liked the simple beige and russet outfit. Very classy. A husky, older man climbed out of the back seat and took the dish she was holding. Leah hesitated for a fraction of a second, then stepped toward the open door.

"Leah!" Jake called. "Excuse me, hon, but you forgot to give me some sheets!"

Hon? Leah straightened and turned to see Jake strolling toward the car. He waved at her. "There are extra sheets on the top shelf of the downstairs bathroom closet. Paul will show you."

"Paul?"

"The sitter."

"Okay, thanks." Jake smiled at the man standing near Leah. No competition. He could tell right away this guy wasn't Leah's type. "Oh, and what about toilet paper?"

He was deliberately being obnoxious. It was almost funny, Leah decided, but not quite. "It's there, too. Help yourself."

She ended the conversation by stepping into the sedan while a man she had never before met held open the car door. She hadn't really expected Patsy would bring a "friend." The man smiled, handed her the platter of eggs and slid onto the back seat. "Thanks," Leah said, feeling a little silly.

"Have a good time," Jake called.

Pat twisted around to look at Leah. Her dark hair was tied in a twist at the nape of her neck, and her blue eyes held questions. "New tenant?"

Leah nodded. "Yes. Hi, Joe," she said to the man behind the wheel. "Thanks for picking me up."

"No problem," Patsy said. "I'd like you to meet Mel Fielding. He's one of our new emergency room doctors and since he's not on duty tonight, I brought him along."

Leah awkwardly shook hands with Mel Fielding. She might murder Patsy if she could get her alone. Leah hated being fixed up. Her friends couldn't seem to believe she wasn't interested in men. She didn't have the time to be interested. With three houses to oversee, a word-processing business and now college classes, she'd be lucky if she had time to sleep. And a six-year-old son with binoculars and a sneaky habit of antagonizing the neighbors would give any mother nightmares.

"I thought you were going to get your car back today," Patsy said.

Leah shook her head. "My old Cadillac has finally died, so I'm car shopping. Anybody have any suggestions?"

"I like my Saab," Mel offered.

Leah tried not to laugh. A Saab. She could probably finance the rest of her education with what one of those cars cost. "I, uh, was thinking of something a little less expensive." Older, too.

"Something used with a few miles left, right?" Joe offered.

Like me, Leah wanted to say, but didn't. Mel might not have a sense of humor. "Right."

"I'll keep my ears open."

Patsy twisted farther around to grin at her best friend. "Who's the new tenant?"

"The man who's renovating the church."

"Too bad you rented the place already," her friend continued. "I talked to an elderly lady at the hospital yesterday who needed a place to live. I don't know if she wanted to be seven miles from town, but I gave her your number."

"I'll be glad to talk to her," Leah said. "Jake only needs the cottage for a couple of months."

"I'd give a lot to see the inside of that church. It must be incredible."

"It is," Leah agreed, thinking of the amount of work Jake Kennedy had left to do.

"You've *seen* it?"

"I took the grand tour this afternoon." Leah looked at

Patsy's astonished expression and grinned. "Jake Kennedy has his work cut out for him."

Patsy's eyebrows arched. "He looked as if he could handle the job."

Leah shrugged and turned to the man beside her. She didn't want to talk about Jake anymore tonight. She'd had her fill of him for one day. "So, Mel, how long have you lived in South County?"

"HAVE DINNER WITH ME TONIGHT."

Leah, busy sponging the inside of the stove in the farmhouse, turned around to see Jake's denim-covered legs. "What?"

He crouched down so that he was on eye level with her, his handsome face only inches away.

"Have dinner with me tonight," he repeated. "Do you like lobster?"

"That's really nice of you, but—"

"Don't say no," he interrupted. "I'm tired of eating alone."

Leah stalled, leaning back on her heels. "Sorry, Jake, but I have to finish cleaning up this house before the girls arrive."

"It's only eleven o'clock."

"After this I have other work to do."

"Like what?"

"Typing. I have a word processor and type papers, mostly for students at the university." Leah rinsed out her sponge in the dishpan and went back to wiping the greasy foam off the walls of the oven.

"Here, Leah," he said, pulling a piece of paper out of his pocket. "I brought the rent check."

"Thanks. Would you set it on the counter?" That was one

problem solved. Now if she could only start shopping for a nice, reliable, economical car.

He tossed the check near the sink and crouched back down to be near Leah. "You're a busy lady."

"I like it that way. Don't you have work to do?"

"Yeah." He grinned. "I started at dawn and lost interest about ten minutes ago."

She couldn't help smiling back at him. "That's not a good sign."

He shrugged. "None of my men work on Sunday, and there's not a lot I can do by myself except straighten up. How was your date last night?"

"It wasn't—" Leah stopped. She didn't have to explain anything to her new tenant. Instead she carefully rinsed out her sponge again.

"Wasn't much fun?" he finished for her. "I can understand that."

"Wasn't a date," Leah stated. "It was a birthday party for a friend."

"How about going out for a quick lunch, then?"

"You don't give up easily, do you?" She grabbed a fistful of paper towels and finished drying the oven. "There," she said, leaning back and shutting the oven door. "That's a job I hate to do."

"What about those self-cleaning things?" His cleaning lady had just pressed a switch.

"They cost money, Jake." She stood, picked up the dishpan and dumped the water into the sink.

"This is a great old house." Jake ran his hand along the wide, pine trim that flanked the doorway. "Show me the rest of it?"

Leah pulled off her yellow rubber gloves and tossed them onto the counter. "Well, all right. It's the kind of house that needs a lot of tender loving care and money. It's been rented for years—my grandmother always said she preferred to live in the smaller house because it was easier to take care of, but I think she only moved because the rent from this place paid the bills. It's been in the family for four generations."

She led him into the sunny dining room, and then to the living room that ran the length of the house. Empty bookshelves lined the fieldstone fireplace, French doors led to a small screened porch, and a wide staircase curved along the opposite wall. The furniture was simple and obviously well used.

"The study's through there—" Leah pointed past the stairs "—and five bedrooms and a bathroom upstairs."

"It's a beauty," Jake said. "You could do a lot with it."

"Like new ceilings and lots of insulation," Leah agreed with a laugh. "You can see why Willie and I don't live here. It costs a small fortune to heat, and the two of us would rattle around in this place."

"You rent it furnished?"

"Just barely. Summer people don't care, and the college kids bring a lot of their own stuff."

He followed her back to the kitchen. "Are you finished?"

"Just about." Leah looked around the sparkling kitchen. All she had left to do was scrub the sink. "The students are bringing their own sheets and blankets, and I finished defrosting the refrigerator Friday."

"Good," Jake said, stepping closer. "I'm thinking about spending the afternoon at the beach. Want to go with me?"

She put on her gloves and grabbed the can of cleanser. "No."

"It's Sunday, a day of rest."

"That's nice," Leah said, hoping he'd get the message as she began to scrub the old, white porcelain sink.

"The tourists are gone. We'll have the whole place to ourselves—you, me and your little spy."

"Sorry, Jake."

He sighed. "You're telling me to bug off."

"Exactly." She smiled at him as he turned to leave. "See you around."

"YOU WANNA BUY EGGS?"

Jake tilted the brim of his baseball cap and opened his eyes. Willie stood beside the couch, hands on his hips, dressed in a Superman outfit. The red cape, looking suspiciously like an old beach towel, hung around his neck. "Didn't your mother teach you to knock before you walk into someone's house?"

Willie shrugged. "This is my mother's house."

"Not while I'm paying the rent." Jake's voice was cheerful. "Where is your mother, anyway?"

"She's workin' at her computer." Willie surveyed the room carefully. Jake figured he was probably looking for evidence.

"Does she know where you are?"

The boy shrugged again, turning his attention back to Jake. "Well?"

"Well, what?" Jake sat up and swung his legs onto the floor. Here Willie wanted someone to talk to, and a few hours ago he couldn't talk Leah into going to the beach, which was probably a good thing. Just because he was lonely on Sundays didn't mean he had to hang out with his workaholic landlady.

"Do you want to buy some eggs?"

"Why? You selling them?"

Willie nodded. "I've got ten hens."

Jake winced, remembering the unfamiliar cackling that

had woken him early this morning. "I've heard them. The coop's next door, isn't it?"

Willie nodded. "I used to have twelve, but a fox ate two of them. At least, I think it was a fox. It could've been a possum because they have really sharp teeth, but I don't know if they eat chickens, do they?"

"How much?"

"The guts were everywhere," he continued. "It was really gross."

"How much?" Jake repeated.

"A dollar a dozen, but you have to give me the carton back."

"It's a deal," Jake said, standing up and pulling his wallet from his pocket. He handed the small boy a dollar bill. "When do I get them?"

"I gotta wash some. I'll be back in a minute."

Jake went into the kitchen and opened the refrigerator. Beer and milk stared back at him, but neither was appealing. The kid would bring eggs; at least he'd cook up an omelet for breakfast tomorrow.

Jake slammed the door shut. Too bad Leah was so stubborn about going out to dinner tonight. He'd grown tired of eating alone and wouldn't mind having a friend to talk to. Pritchard's Corner seemed a pretty quiet place, and although the entire area was a resort town, the women he'd seen were either pushing strollers or holding hands with their husbands. It was a good thing he didn't want to get involved with women right now, because from what he'd seen, the entire adult population of Rhode Island was married.

Willie appeared at the screen door. "Do I hafta knock now?"

"Yeah," Jake replied, determined to teach the kid some

manners. When the banging on the door stopped, he yelled, "Come in!"

Willie stepped inside and handed him the carton. "Don't forget, I got to have the carton back."

He set it on the counter. "No problem."

"Where are you going?"

"Back to work." Jake grabbed his gloves off the table. He might as well accomplish something besides taking a nap today.

"Can I come?"

"No."

"Why not?"

"Last time I heard, you were grounded." Jake ushered the child out the open screen door. "Remember?"

Willie didn't look too concerned. "It prob'ly wouldn't count if I was with you. And there are too many girls around here."

Jake shook his head. *Nice try, kid.* "No. Go tell your mom she wants you."

"I know that joke," Willie said, watching Jake step outside and lock the door. "I'm six."

"Congratulations." Jake strode through the yard, content to escape from the child's company. He noted several unfamiliar cars parked in the driveway. Leah's college kids must have arrived.

Willie kept up with him, hurrying to match Jake's long strides. "My friends watched you, too. Nobody else believes in Superman, but I do."

"Do you think that's smart?"

"I don't care."

Jake stopped at the gravel that marked the beginning of the driveway and looked helplessly at the belligerent child.

"Look, kid," Jake began, searching for the right words. "I don't care if you believe in Superman or the tooth fairy—

you can believe anything you want, but believe this. I can't leap tall buildings or fly or see through walls. I'm not Superman. Got it?"

Willie's eyes widened. A stubborn expression crossed his face and his hands balled into fists at his side. "You shouldn't lie."

Jake hesitated. The kid was right on target with that one. Why not tell him about the television show and forget it? Because the word would be out, he'd be connected with *Fascination*, and the precious privacy he treasured so highly would go right down the drain. Surely he could fake out one small boy—eight years of acting ought to have taught him something.

Jake guiltily assumed his most sincere expression. "I'm not lying, Willie," he said, willing the boy to believe his words. After all, he wasn't really Superman, only the guy who'd made it successfully through the casting call. "I'm nobody's hero."

"You wear blue underwear," Willie countered.

"I know."

Leah's voice rang from the open window near where the man and boy stood in a stalemate. "William!"

Jake peered toward the window, but couldn't see through the screen. Had Leah heard the entire conversation? *Good*, he thought with satisfaction. *She needs to know how strange her son is.* Jake turned back to the boy, but Willie sprinted a hundred-yard dash around the chicken coop before his mother appeared on the porch steps.

Leah frowned. "Where is he?"

"Beats me." Jake grinned. He wished he'd had a stopwatch—the kid should be encouraged to go out for track.

She put her hands on her hips. "Was he wearing that red cape again?"

"Yeah. Don't all egg salesmen dress like that?"

Leah's lips softened into a smile, and she swept her copper hair away from her face. "He's bothering you again." It was stated as fact.

Jake nodded. "I can handle it."

"You shouldn't have to."

She was right, Jake knew. Hadn't that been what he'd felt all along? But somehow, standing here looking at the woman in the yellow sundress, it didn't seem all that important. He gripped his work gloves a little tighter. "True. Just keep him away from the church. I don't want him to get hurt."

Leah nodded. "I'm trying." She paused before continuing. "Are you going to work?"

"Yeah. I changed my mind and decided I could get a few things done this afternoon. You change your mind about the beach?"

She smiled and shook her head. "No. I'm working, too."

"Your renters checked in, right?"

"Yes, an hour ago," Leah answered. "Six gorgeous young women. Don't say I didn't warn you."

"Oh, I can take care of myself," Jake drawled, but when he tore his gaze away from Leah's sparkling, hazel eyes, he wondered if he'd overestimated himself.

THE GUY WAS just an ordinary carpenter, Leah told herself.

"Ordinary, ordinary, ordinary," she muttered. Maybe if she said it enough times, she just might believe it. Leah squinted at the green numbers displayed on the monitor, then double-checked them against the figures written on the yellow paper beside the keyboard. Two mistakes. It might be a good idea to keep her mind on her work instead of wondering about her new tenant.

Disgusted with herself, Leah quickly corrected the errors before continuing to the next section of the financial statement for Paul's mother. Her fingers flew over the keys, the clicking of the soft plastic the only sound in the house.

Moments later, after Leah stopped to turn the page, her gaze drifted toward the window and the quiet yard beyond. The college girls had piled into a car and left, presumably to stock up on groceries. They'd seemed like a nice group of kids this year, quiet and mature. Leah hadn't seen Jake return, and Willie had taken his box of small, metal cars outside to a dirt "racetrack" underneath the shade of the huge maple next to the coop. With Jake gone, Leah figured Willie would remain content to play by himself. Without wearing a red cape.

She glanced at her watch—four-thirty. Her aching shoulders hinted it might be time to stop typing. She pressed the Save key and, leaving the computer equipment running, pushed back her chair and grabbed the newspaper off the couch. It was definitely time for a cold drink and another stab at examining the lengthy classified ads in the automobile section of the Providence Sunday *Journal*. She'd looked through them once, and didn't even know where to begin. There were certainly disadvantages to having an open mind.

After turning back to her desk and grabbing a red marking pen, she ducked into her son's room and peeked at him from the window. A hundred feet away, he was the picture of little-boy activity, digging in the dirt and shaping mountains as metal cars lay scattered around him. Thank goodness. Even Jake Kennedy couldn't find fault with the kid now. What did he know about raising children, anyway?

Leah headed for the kitchen, newspaper still in hand. Conquer the car, she decided. A priority of major importance. A whole new education in "buying used." She spread the paper over the table and hunched over it, willing the ad for the perfect car to leap off the pages and into her line of vision. What brand? How old? "Loaded" sounded good. That probably meant radio, air-conditioning and power everything. Local phone numbers would be a plus, too.

"Hello?" a voice rumbled from the living room.

A deep voice. Jake.

"Coming," Leah answered, reluctantly leaving the kitchen to see Jake standing behind the screen door. "Yes?"

He stepped inside, a frown creasing the model-perfect features. "There's a chicken on my bed."

"What?"

He stepped closer, keeping his voice low. "There's a *chicken*. On my *bed*."

"Why are you whispering?"

He looked surprised, then spoke louder. "I sneaked home through the cemetery and over the wall, so your son wouldn't see me until I'd locked myself in the house. I made it, too, until I got inside and saw that damn hen."

"And you sneaked over here? Willie's playing near the chicken coop—he must have seen you."

Jake shook his head. "I cut between your house and mine. Could you get that bird out of my house before it sh—messes all over the floor?"

Leah tried not to smile. "Certainly."

Jake followed her outside to his cottage. Willie hurried toward them, a fat, auburn hen cradled in his arms.

"What's going on?" Leah asked.

The child looked panicked. "She didn't mean it. I'm giving her a ride home."

"A ride out of my house, I think," Jake grumbled. "To where?"

Willie's eyes grew larger, and he hastened to reassure the tall man standing before him. "Alien's ready to go back to the coop now."

Jake's gaze shifted to the content hen. "Alien?"

Leah turned to him, knowing this was a lost cause. "She has two different-colored feet, so Willie named her Alien. She also likes to roam around the yard and visit other places."

"Well, I don't want her visiting me anymore."

"It's my fault. I should have warned you," Leah said, following him to his door. "This screen door is pretty light, and the chickens sometimes try to push their way inside." She pointed to a hook near Jake's shoulder. "You have to close the latch when you leave."

"I'll remember that." He pushed open the door. "I wondered why this door opened in instead of out."

Leah shrugged. She'd never given it much thought. "It's always been that way."

He stepped gingerly across the floor. "No sign of a, uh, mess."

"Fine," Leah said, ready to escape back to her newspaper.

"Leah?"

She turned around, her hand on the doorknob. *Now what?*

"What about this?" A brown egg had been deposited in a soft hollow of the bedspread. Jake cradled it in his large hand and held it toward Leah.

"Finders keepers?"

The corners of his mouth twitched. "All right. But if you don't mind, I'll fix that door."

"Be my guest," she answered lightly. He could hammer away, if that would make him happy and keep the chickens out of his house.

Leah had no sooner settled herself with the newspaper again when she heard Jake's voice outside the door once more.

"Leah?" he called.

"Come in." She sighed. What could have gone wrong now?

He peered around the corner of the kitchen. "Save me a trip back to the church," he said, "and let me use your phone. I need to order a pizza."

Pizza. The word created visions of melting cheese, crunchy pepperoni and thick, filling crust. "Pizza?" She almost drooled.

"Yeah." He pulled a slip of paper from his shirt pocket. "I eat a lot of it," he added unnecessarily.

Leah remembered the box on his kitchen counter last night. "Like every day?"

He chuckled. "Almost. I try different places— I'm looking for the perfect pizza, sort of an unofficial survey."

"What happens when you find it?"

"Then I'm going to start searching for the perfect cheesecake. I already found the best fish and chips in the state." He nodded at the paper. "What are you looking for?"

"A car." She pointed to the wall phone hanging by the refrigerator. "Help yourself."

"Great." He picked up the receiver and dialed. "You want to share a large pepperoni?"

"From where?"

He named a place in Narragansett, and Leah hesitated. It was against her better judgment to have a meal with this man, but she didn't feel like cooking. To be sure, the shelves were lined with cookbooks of all kinds, and she loved to try new recipes. Her grandmother had taught her how to bake and her mother how to make gravy. She'd taught herself the rest. But it was Sunday and it was hot, and she had more work ahead of her than she wanted to think about.

"That's a good place," she said slowly. "It might be your winner."

"Are we on, then?"

"Okay."

He grinned, then spoke into the phone. "Yeah. Kennedy. Thanks." He hung up the phone and leaned against the wall. "It'll be ready in about twenty minutes. Want to ride over with me?"

Tempting. Very tempting, but Leah shook her head. "I'd better stick with the ads."

Jake walked to the table and leaned over the opened newspaper. "Why are you looking for a new car?"

"Mine died." Jake's strong forearms were inches away from Leah's face as he braced himself on the tabletop. She felt trapped.

"What kind of car are you looking for?"

"Uh, something dependable and cheap."

He raised his eyebrows. "As in, 'Grandmother drove it to church on Sundays'?"

"Exactly. I had an old Cadillac that my grandmother did drive to church on Sundays, but Gibson advised junking it instead of spending the money to fix it up."

"Too bad." Jake bent closer to the paper, his face perilously close to Leah's shoulder. "You want another old Cadillac?"

"I, uh, don't think so." She leaned slightly away from him. "Something smaller would be easier to park and get better gas mileage."

"Like a Honda or a Ford Escort?"

"I suppose." She wished he'd move away a few inches. "Maybe not that small— I don't know."

Jake straightened and took a step backward. "Come on, I'll run you past a used-car lot in town before we get the pizza and show you the differences."

"You don't have to do that."

"Look," he said, his gray eyes darkening. "I'll be glad to help you out. I know you can't possibly admit you should ask for help, but you should try it sometime. It might not be as hard as you think."

Leah was silent for a minute. "You're right. I hate asking for help."

"Why the hell is it such a big deal?"

She looked away from his scrutiny. There was no sense explaining to a perfect stranger that she'd taken care of other people her entire life, from her sick mother to her aging grandmother and, of course, Willie. She'd been taught to get it herself or go without. "I guess it's a New England tradition. You know, stiff upper lip and nose to the grindstone?"

"Sounds painful."

"I guess it is," she said, meeting his twinkling gaze.

"I'm your neighbor. Aren't neighbors helpful in New England?"

She nodded.

"Well?" he demanded impatiently. "Grab the kid and get in the truck." The smile he shot her was devastating. "Unless you want to walk to school next week."

Leah met his smile with a shy one of her own. "No, thanks."

IT WAS TURNING OUT better than he'd expected. She'd left the kid with a neighbor, which meant he and Leah had the front seat of the truck to themselves. Which meant steady conversation. Which meant no interruptions, except that the lady wasn't much of a talker, so there wasn't much conversation to interrupt.

That was okay, too, Jake decided, turning the car off the highway and onto the street that led to the used-car lot. A shiny array of used cars was usually lined up near the main road, and today was no exception.

Jake slowed down the truck as they neared the entrance. "Any color?"

Leah looked surprised as he turned the wheel and the truck bounced into the parking lot. "What does color have to do with anything?"

He shrugged. "I thought you might have a color you hate. It eliminates looking at those cars."

She looked at him as if he'd lost his mind, then shook her head. "No, no color preferences."

He switched the ignition off and opened the door. "Let's go kick a few tires."

"Do people really do that?"

"Yeah. It's tradition." Jake went around to open the door for her, but she'd already hopped down onto the ground, so he had to be content to walk beside her.

"None of them have prices." She sighed. "It's the price that matters the most."

"That's a starting point, I suppose."

"All of these cars look fine, except maybe that one." She pointed to a rusty station wagon that looked as if it had been parked next to the ocean a few thousand times too many.

"You really should shop around and get an idea what the best deal is."

"I don't have time for it. It's not that I don't want the best deal, it's just that I don't have days and weeks to find it."

Jake guided her toward a silver Subaru sedan and peered through the window at the odometer. "Eighty-three thousand miles. The interior's in good shape, too."

A salesman came out of the office building and walked over to them. "That's a real sweet one," he said. "Just got it in a few days ago, on trade. Would you two like to take it for a spin?"

"How much is it?" Leah asked.

He named a price higher than Jake would have guessed.

"Guess not," Leah answered. "Do you have anything a thousand dollars less than that?"

"Tell you what, you take this for a test drive and then we'll see if we can make a deal. I'll go get the keys while you see if there's anything else here that looks good." At Leah's hesitant nod, he turned and went back into the sales office.

Jake kicked the tires. "They're not old."

"It's the right size." Leah roamed among the other cars but returned to the Subaru. It appeared to fit her requirements the best. "But I've never driven anything but a Cadillac."

The man returned and unlocked the driver's door. "Here you go, folks. You trading in the truck?"

"No," Jake said. "No trade-in."

He looked disappointed. "No matter—we'll work something out if the lady likes the Subaru." He hung a temporary license plate on the back of the car.

Jake didn't like the way the man leered at Leah. Sure, she looked beautiful in the yellow dress, with her long hair curling against her bare shoulders. The tan legs were hidden because the dress was long, but her sunglasses gave her a mysterious air that would tempt any man with two good eyes.

"All right," Jake said, speaking before Leah could say anything. "Come on, hon, let's take it for a ride and see if you like it." He turned to the salesman. "We'll be back in about fifteen minutes."

Leah frowned. There was that "hon" stuff again.

The salesman looked at his watch. "Are you people local?"

"Pritchard's Corner," Jake said.

"That's not too far away. I'm closing in ten minutes, so I'll let you keep it overnight if you want. That way you can get an idea if you like it. Leave me some identification, bring the car back in the morning and we'll talk."

Leah looked back at the car. It was tempting, oh, so tempting. The right size, and possibly the right price. She'd check with Steve at Gibson's in the morning and have him look at the car to see if it could last another thirty thousand miles. "Fine," she agreed.

Jake was disgusted with himself as he drove toward Narragansett. He'd wanted a few minutes alone with his lovely landlady, and instead he was alone in his truck while Leah followed behind him, alone in her little car. She'd looked happy about it, too, as she'd slid behind the wheel of the sedan.

Just his luck. He'd tried to engineer some time with her so he could be charming—just some female companionship, nothing more—and perhaps share a meal with something other than a cardboard box or the hood of his truck. A little conversation while riding through town would have been pleasant.

He looked into his rearview mirror. Leah waved, and Jake signalled a right signal, preparing to turn into the shopping center as soon as the light turned green. He'd pick up the pizza and follow Leah home, enjoy a little companionship over dinner, then go home and see if any other hens had trespassed upon his new home. It wouldn't take X-ray vision to find out.

4

LEAH LIKED the way the Subaru handled as it zipped along behind Jake's truck. *Wheels.* How much better could life get?

Maybe having Jake around wasn't so bad, after all. Maybe he really was a pleasant carpenter who couldn't help being handsome, charming and demanding. He could ease up on the charm, Leah decided, as she saw him look at her in his rearview mirror. She waved politely, then watched the truck's right taillight blink. Charm soon wore thin.

She followed him into the parking lot and pulled into the empty space beside the truck. The engine purred softly before Leah reluctantly turned off the ignition.

"Well?" Jake slammed the door shut and walked around the back of the truck. Lean hips, tight denim and broad shoulders stepped toward her. "What do you think?"

Leah cleared her throat. "I guess I like it so far."

Jake bent over and leaned against the car, blocking Leah from opening the door and filling the opened window with his handsome, well-planed face. "How did it steer?"

"Fine." His gray eyes were much too piercing and much too close. Leah reached for the door handle and pulled, hoping Jake would get the hint and move away. "It's a lot smaller than I'm used to."

He backed up and opened the car door for her. "Check

with Gibson's in the morning and see if they'll go over the engine for you."

"I will." Leah remembered to pull the key from the ignition, then stepped onto the pavement to stand next to Jake. The man made her feel like a queen—all right, a nervous queen—just by holding open a door. Why should he have this effect on her? As the door clicked shut behind her, Jake lifted his hand to take hers, as if holding hands was as natural to him as breathing. Leah pretended not to notice the gesture and his arm dropped back to his side.

"You shouldn't buy the first car you see," he said.

"Why not?" Obviously he'd never been totally without transportation.

"You should shop around."

"The salesman seemed willing to deal."

He snorted. "They all are. That's their job."

"I'll see what he has to say."

Jake looked down at her as they stopped to let a car pass. 'What a reasonable woman you are."

"You make it sound like an insult."

He smiled his movie-star smile. "Lady," he began, the title sounding too much like an endearment, "I would never insult you, especially not when we're about to have dinner together."

"Sharing a pizza out of a box isn't having dinner together."

"Call me optimistic."

Leah didn't know what to say to that. They crossed the street together and stepped onto the sidewalk in front of the restaurant, where Jake opened the door for her.

"What would you call it?" he asked.

"Convenience."

He ushered her through the door, his smile one of

amused tolerance that made her want to kick his denim-covered shins. "Convenience?" he echoed. "Why's that?"

"I'm paying my half, saving gas, saving time...you get the picture." A line of people waited near the cash register, and Leah inhaled the warm air scented with yeast and garlic.

"So?"

Leah frowned. She tried to come up with another good reason as they approached the take-out counter. "Isn't that enough?"

"Nope."

She followed him to the counter, where he had no trouble catching the eye of a heavily made-up teenager.

"Can I help you?" The girl looked overwhelmed.

Jake nodded. "A large pepperoni for uh, Kennedy. Is it ready?"

"Yeah, I think so," she said. "I'll check." She turned away to read the names on the boxes piled up on the ovens.

Leah waited next to Jake, wondering at the brief hesitation before Jake had said his name. A trunk with Kent on the side, Willie had said. How would Jake explain that? *You're getting as bad as your son,* she told herself.

The waitress returned and set the pizza box on the counter in front of them. "Anything else?"

"What?"

Jake glanced down at her. "Do you want drinks? Or ice cream?"

"No. I have all that at home."

The girl hesitated at the cash register. "All set, then?"

"Yeah," Jake said, pulling his wallet from the back pocket of his jeans. "I guess we are."

"That'll be $6.72." The girl punched numbers into the machine.

"Here," Leah offered, unzipping her bag and grabbing her billfold. "I'm paying half, remember?"

Jake sighed. "I remember. It's not necessary, but I guess I didn't expect it any other way."

"Good." She put her money onto the counter and slid it toward Jake. He added to it without further comment and the waitress took the bills, then handed the change to Jake. He picked up the pizza and followed Leah to the door.

"You're a hard woman to take to dinner, Mrs. Lang."

"Miss," she corrected, opening the door and holding it for him, "and I thought you were going to call me Leah." As soon as she said it, Leah was sorry. Why had she opened her big mouth?

"I was," he said, seeming pleased with himself as he walked beside her to the car. "I am."

This time he followed her. Every time she glanced into the mirror she saw the red truck. Leah fiddled with the unfamiliar radio dials and managed not to exceed the speed limit by more than five miles per hour. When she reached her driveway, Jake was still close behind.

"Still like it?" he called.

"It's great," she declared, climbing out of the car and standing back to admire it. "I just hope I can afford it."

"It's what you need, I guess, but why don't you let me take you car shopping again? Tomorrow afternoon, maybe?"

Leah shook her head. "I don't have the time. Classes start tomorrow and I'm getting a ride with the girls next door." She nodded toward the big house. "If Gibson's says this little car is okay, then I'll buy it if I get the price I need."

"Don't be afraid to bargain."

"I won't." She saw Willie carefully cross the street. "Let's eat. You must be starving." As Jake followed her, Leah realized that sharing a pizza meant sharing a meal, too. Another half hour with Jake.

Willie quickly caught up with them as they entered the house. "We're gonna eat together?"

"Yep," his mother said. "Right after you wash your hands."

Willie looked as if he wanted to argue, but hurried to the sink instead. "Pizza again? Wow!"

"This is your lucky week," Leah said, grabbing paper plates from the cupboard near the sink and tossing them onto the center of the table.

Willie was clearly awestruck. "No kidding."

No kidding, Jake repeated silently. He was making progress. At least he was in Leah's house, sharing dinner. Better—much better—than eating alone. Of course, one never knew when a hen would drop in. Maybe he wouldn't be in such a hurry to fix that door. Alien's offerings were a ready-made topic of conversation.

"Sit down, Jake," Leah offered, opening the refrigerator. "The pizza's getting cold."

He did as he was told, moving his chair slightly away from the curious child.

"What do you want to drink?" She rummaged through the shelves. "Diet cola or milk or, uh, possibly the oldest bottle of beer in Rhode Island history?"

"I'll risk the beer," he replied, wondering what man had left it in Leah's refrigerator.

"Want a glass?"

"No, thanks." She handed it to him, then poured a glass of milk for the kid before taking a can of soda to the table for herself. She dropped a handful of silverware onto the table. "Just in case anybody needs a fork," she said as she sat down in the chair across from Jake's and slid the napkin holder over to him.

He took a couple of white paper napkins and handed one to Willie.

"Is pizza the only thing you eat?" the child asked.

"William..." Leah's voice held a warning.

"I like fish, too," Jake said, looking at the boy. "Do you?"

He shrugged. "Sorta."

Leah picked out a piece of pizza, dragged it onto her plate and struggled to resist the urge to question her new tenant. She'd like to solve the mystery, and there definitely was one. What if he was a serial killer? What if she turned on that television show about unsolved mysteries and saw an old picture of Jake staring back at her? She didn't care for the thought, Leah decided, glancing across the table at Mr. Handsome, helping himself to another piece of pizza.

"Our Town Pizza might win." He lifted one corner of the triangle to his lips.

"Win?" she echoed, confused.

Jake stopped before taking a bite. "The best pizza contest, remember? The unofficial Kennedy survey."

"Wow," Willie breathed. "Can I be a judge?"

Jake winked at Leah before turning back to the child. "Maybe."

Willie shot a brave look at his mother, then asked, "What'd you do when you were a kid, Jake?"

"Almost the same things you do," he answered.

Willie persisted. "Like what?"

Jake shrugged. "Climbed trees, rode my bike, hung out with my friends." He thought for a second, then lied through his teeth. Old Man Wilkie had spent more than a few hours chasing boys off his farm. "I didn't spy on anyone."

"But—" Willie stopped, catching the look his mother gave him.

"But," Jake added, feeling guilty about the lie, "we got

into our share of trouble. My father took my bike away for a month one time."

Leah relaxed a little more. Her instincts told her Jake was a nice enough guy. Just because he made her nervous was no reason to suspect him of something illegal or mysterious. "Where are you from, Jake?" She told herself she was only being polite.

"New York, remember?"

"I meant where in New York."

"Oh. Watertown."

Leah broke the moment's silence. "And did you build houses there?"

"My father did."

Which was what he'd said that evening at the church. That didn't explain what Jake Kennedy did for a living. All right, so he wasn't exactly brimming with information about himself. Maybe he was shy. "It must have been a wonderful thing to work in your father's business."

"I didn't always. I worked in advertising for a few years, until other things came along."

"Other things?" Leah told herself it was normal to be curious about the person who would spend the rest of the fall in the house next to hers.

Jake nodded. "Nothing important."

"Do you remodel houses or build new ones sometimes?"

"Both, but my father loved doing the old, historic places." Jake took a drink of bitter beer, then smiled at the worried expression in Leah's eyes. "Is this Twenty Questions we're playing?"

Her cheeks flushed a soft rose color. "Yes."

"Would you like references, Leah? I can give you as many as you want, plus you can call my mother in Florida or my cousin in Arizona."

Her sigh of relief was audible. "I'd like that." She should

have asked for references earlier, but she had been too distracted by her financial worries. Now that she had realized her mistake, she was glad he was so willing to ease her mind.

"Now what?"

Leah looked up at him once again. "Yes?"

"Is there anything else on your mind, or can I finish this piece of pizza?"

"You can finish that and have three more. Half of this pizza is yours, remember." He'd paid for half; she should let him enjoy it. "You can give me the names and numbers later."

Willie tugged on Jake's arm to get his attention. "Why'd your dad take your bike away?"

Jake chuckled. "I'd better not tell you. It might give you ideas."

Leah reached for another cheesy slice of pizza, deciding to use her fork and avoid making more of a mess. Maybe the mysterious Mr. Kennedy wasn't such a mystery, after all. And he was right—her son had enough ideas without hearing any more.

"SYBIL LEAVES LOVER COLE-D."

Jake did a double take, hoping he'd misread the screaming headline. But there it was, on one of the weekly supermarket tabloids, hanging from its rack by the checkout counter at Stop 'n' Shop.

"Sybil Leaves Lover COLE-D."

It was there, all right. In black and white. On cheap paper. On the cover of *True Gossip*. Jake clutched a couple of boxes of doughnuts and a can of coffee and stepped closer. The large picture of Sybil Cole was not a flattering one. The sexy pout that intrigued millions of viewers every Thursday night was missing, replaced by an expression even the kindest fan would have to call "bitchy."

But it was the caption underneath the picture that made him groan. Jeffrey Kent Leaves Lover Fuming.

Damn. The express counter wasn't very express this morning. He wanted to turn around and run, but there were two people behind him now and he was third in line.

He looked at the picture again. Sybil would be infuriated by the photograph, Jake knew. That alone would have made him laugh, except his name was mentioned, too. Linked with Sybil, no less. Jake glanced around casually, thankful he'd worn his mirrored sunglasses. Would anyone possibly connect the actor who'd played the smooth and sophisticated Jason Masters with Jake Kennedy, a scruffy carpenter holding a can of coffee?

Jake took a deep breath, the kind of relaxing strategy he'd used before stepping onto the stage. No one was going to recognize him. No one.

This was a lousy time to run out of coffee. Some of the crew needed the extra caffeine to deal with weekend hangovers. Jake fidgeted in line. Thank goodness, he didn't do that kind of partying anymore. After he'd hit thirty, the pain of the morning after took all the fun out of the night before. He'd always been good at avoiding bars, drunks and crowds.

The elderly woman in front of him sneezed, and someone else in line murmured the obligatory "Bless you."

Jake shifted uneasily.

"Sir?"

Jake walked forward, tossing the items onto the conveyor belt before digging his wallet from his jeans. He'd breathe a lot easier once he got out of the store and away from the magazine rack. *Damn Sybil.* She'd probably paid someone to leak the ridiculous story. The opening night of the season was in two weeks. His gorgeous costar was no fool. She wanted ratings and knew how to get them.

Once out of the store, Jake strode across the parking lot to his truck. He'd thought *Fascination* and Jeffrey Kent were behind him, and glanced into the mirror to reassure himself.

His hair was longer now, shaded differently. The pants were denim, the shirts cheap. Rarely seen in anything but green contact lenses and beige, designer sport jackets, Jeffrey Kent had bared his shoulder blades and bedded the show's horny women to the delight of *Fascination*'s devoted fans. His character had had more affairs than he could keep track of, heightening his appeal for the mostly female audience. But that was over now. The man with "the most famous back on television" had turned that famous back on Hollywood.

Jake climbed into his truck and gunned the engine. There was no way he'd let his past intrude on the peaceful future he was determined to enjoy in Rhode Island. Pritchard's Corner was his home now— Hollywood could go on without him. After *Fascination*'s season opener, they'd never even miss him. He'd be just another has-been, alive only in reruns. A frown creased his face as he jammed the gears into Reverse. Alive in reruns, just like Superman.

"COULD YOU *PLEASE* get him out of there?"

Jake's aggravated voice cut into Leah's concentration, and she looked up from the keyboard to see him standing inside the front door of the living room. "Out of where?"

"The tree."

She should have known the peace of the past two weeks couldn't last forever. Although the work was hard, classes were going smoothly and she liked what she was learning. Willie seemed content with his first-grade teacher, and her new Subaru continued to start in the morning. Only Jake and Willie couldn't get along. "What's wrong with him being up in the tree?"

"He's back with the binoculars again."

"He's bird-watching," she countered.

"And I'm Sylvester Stallone."

"Glad to meet you."

"Very funny." He didn't look amused.

"Is there any way we can work this out?"

Not with True Gossip on my case. Jake sighed, reminding himself to stay in control. His lips twisted into a wry smile. "Barring jumping off the roof of the chicken coop to prove I can't fly, I can't think of anything."

Leah didn't return the smile. Behind on her reading for Psych class, she had to finish writing this history paper, then needed to type Paul's book report before the weekend was over. If she was going to take Willie to the football game tonight, she needed to get back to work. She swiveled around to face her guest. "I can't believe he's bothering you that much, Jake."

Jake sat down uninvited on the couch. "He isn't. I'm just edgy."

Leah's brows rose. "Problems with the job?"

"Yeah, and Alien left another gift on my bed."

"I thought you were going to fix the door."

"I forgot."

"I can pick up a lock for you Monday on my way home from school."

"No." Jake shook his head. "Forget it."

Leah waited, but Jake didn't say anything more. "Is there anything else?"

"Your son invited me to dinner tomorrow night."

"He did?"

Jake hid a smile. "I figured he didn't tell you about it."

"That's okay," Leah said, fiddling with her pencil. "I should have thought of it myself, to pay you back for helping me with the car."

"You don't have to. That wasn't such a big deal."

"It was to me."

He shrugged, then stretched out his long legs. "I'm not doing anything tomorrow night. Are you?"

Leah thought quickly. Tomorrow was Saturday. If she got up early and did most of her studying in the morning while Willie watched cartoons, she'd have time in the afternoon to buy groceries and cook. "Then come for dinner."

He hesitated. "Well, if you're sure..."

"I am," she said quickly. She hoped she sounded sincere. "And I'll talk to Willie again."

Jake stood. "Okay. Guess I'll get back to work." He opened the door, then stopped. "What can I bring?"

"Nothing."

"Ice cream?"

"Nothing."

"Wine?"

Stubborn man. "You don't have to bring anything."

"Red or white?"

"Either."

He shrugged and went out the door, letting it bang shut behind him. Leah sighed. Just because the man was truly gorgeous didn't mean she had the time or energy to appreciate having him live next door. Still, she mused, thinking of his charcoal eyes and the dark lashes that fringed them, the guy was good to look at. Superman. Who would have thought a guy like that would end up right in her own backyard?

"CHICKEN ENCHILADAS."

"Hours of preparation."

"Sweet and sour pork."

"If he likes Chinese."

"Tacos."

"Too informal."

"Chicken and artichoke casserole?"

"What about a simple roast beef? Joe always likes that, especially now that he's learned how to make it himself."

Leah continued to flip through the selections in her chipped, metal recipe box. It had been much too long since she'd cooked anything truly edible. It might be fun to see if she could still whip up a decent meal, one with over four ingredients.

"I can't decide," she said into the receiver cradled against her ear.

"Why are you worrying about it so much?" Patsy questioned. "He's not exactly the president of the United States."

"I know." She pulled out a card with faded handwriting along the top. "What about that chicken casserole with the rice and zucchini? Didn't I make it for you once?"

"Um, I think so. Did you bring it to the Labor Day thing last year?"

Leah nodded, then realized her friend couldn't see her. "Uh-huh. I still have zucchini from the garden."

"Then make that. Give him garlic bread and a dessert and everything will be fine."

"I hope so."

"Why wouldn't it be? You're a good cook. Have more faith in yourself."

"I'm not trying to impress him."

"Could've fooled me."

"Really, I'm not." Leah winced. Why was she going to all this trouble, then? "I hope he eats fast. I don't have time for this," she wailed.

"Having a man in your life is not the end of the world."

Leah flipped to the dessert section. "I never said it was."

"Did you see Oprah on Friday?"

"Why? Did she cook?"

"Uh-uh. The show was on women and their sexuality."

"Oh, Lord. That again."

"No, it was great. A male psychologist talked about multiple orgasms."

"What did he know about it?"

"He was a wonderful-looking man. A little like a young Tom Selleck. He's probably contributed to a few orgasms in his lifetime, although he wasn't as handsome as your carpenter."

Leah shut the lid of the recipe box, ignoring the "your carpenter" remark. "Dessert will be brownies, with ice cream and chocolate sauce. I'll keep it simple."

"You do that, Leah." Pat chuckled. "When you're a therapist, are you going to study multiple orgasms?"

Leah laughed. "Sure. Every night. And then, if I can still walk, I'll be on the Oprah Winfrey show before you know it."

"Good." Pat giggled. "Make sure Jake's on the panel with you. That guy's too gorgeous to keep in Pritchard's Corner."

"WHAT DO YOU THINK HE'LL EAT?" Willie asked, a worried expression on his small face. He watched his mother open a can of green chilies.

"I had this discussion with Mrs. Farrel yesterday," Leah answered. "Jake'll eat whatever I give him."

"Because in the movie I didn't see him eat anything like green stuff," he said, pointing to the can.

"Don't start."

"He didn't eat anything. Maybe hamburgers. Can we rent *Superman I* again? Can we have hamburgers?"

"No. And no. We're having chicken casserole."

He shrugged. "It doesn't look too good."

"Thank you, Chef Lang." Leah remained unperturbed. She gave him a good-natured grin and stooped to grab a casserole dish from the back of a cabinet. She wiped the dust off it with a quick swipe of the dish towel, then set it on the counter. She'd surprised herself by having a good time, although getting up at five this morning had given her a good start on the day. It was only three o'clock now— she'd be unconscious by seven if she didn't drink another pot of coffee. After all, she had to entertain Superman to-night. Jake probably wouldn't stay long. He had to work early in the morning, as he did every day. She usually heard his truck pull out of the driveway around six.

"I dunno about this." Willie, eyed the casserole dish with distrust.

"If you want to stay in the kitchen, make yourself useful and set the table. Use the blue place mats in the bottom drawer."

"Why can't we use the fancy stuff?"

"Like what?" What would a six-year-old boy think was fancy?

"The shiny forks."

"I don't think tonight is the night to use the silver, Willie. That's for special occasions, like a holiday."

"Do we hafta use this stuff?" He held up a couple of patchwork place mats Leah had created in her sewing days, when Willie was a baby.

"No, I guess we don't." She resolved to buy some new ones. Her son might have the right idea. There was such a thing as too informal, she supposed. "There should be a ta-blecloth in there somewhere if you keep looking."

He rummaged through the drawer. "Got it!"

Leah wondered why she'd gone along with her son's idea to invite Jake to dinner. Not that she'd been consulted, though Jake had offered her a way to get out of it. Spending a Saturday night with Jake was too much like a date. And something told her that dating this man would be a mistake. She wasn't immune to the fact that he was attracted to her. She'd seen the appreciative look in his eyes when he thought she hadn't noticed. She wasn't stupid. Just because she didn't date didn't mean she'd forgotten what it was like to have a man notice she was breathing the same air.

"Do you think he eats a lot?"

"Are you hinting I might not make enough food?"

"What's for dessert?"

"Who says there's dessert?"

"Mom!"

Leah relented, telling him what she'd planned while she removed a pan from the stove.

"Anybody would like that, don't ya think?"

"I sure do," Leah agreed, spreading fluffy, steaming rice over the bottom of the glass dish. "Even a superhero would have to be impressed."

"Yeah." Willie sighed, daring a look in his mother's direction. "But I ate all the chocolate stuff."

"You mean the sauce? All of it?"

He nodded. "Me and Greg made chocolate milk."

Leah remembered the mess in the kitchen from that particular after-school snack. "Guess we go back to the store, then."

"We?" The dismay in his voice was evident.

"We." She'd better go now, while there was still time. She put down her spoon, deciding to leave everything on the counter until she returned, and wiped her hands on the towel that hung near the sink.

"Now?"

"As soon as I find the car keys." She grabbed her purse off the kitchen chair, found the clump of keys underneath it, and followed Willie into the living room. "You cleaned," she said, noticing the usual clutter was missing. "It looks great."

"Yeah," he announced, a look of pride on his face. "I put all the G.I. Joe guys under the couch."

"Whatever works." Leah looked at her watch and hurried toward the door. "Come on, pal. We have three hours till the main event. Let's go."

The driveway was packed with cars, and a young college woman in scanty shorts and a cutoff shirt jogged up the driveway.

"Hi, Will!" She smiled at the boy. "Getting ready for tonight?"

"Yeah. It's gonna be neat."

Leah looked at her son and whispered. "What's she talking about?"

"Don't mind me," Ellen panted. "It's just that Will here—" she affectionately tousled the boy's hair "—told us all about Superman coming to dinner." She winked at Leah. "I have to admit, Leah, we're all a little envious. He's quite a hunk, isn't he?"

"I suppose," Leah fibbed, looking at her tenant's trim body. Maybe she should consider taking up jogging. Someday. When she had some spare time.

"A little old for us," Ellen suggested, her long, dark hair swinging against her shoulders. "But just right for you."

"I don't think we should talk—"

"Hi, Leah! Hi, Will!" Another girl stepped out of the large house, her arm cradling a basket of laundry. "How's it going?"

"Great, Nancy!" Willie waved. "He's coming tonight."

"What are you, the town crier?" Leah muttered.

Nancy, a tall blonde, walked closer and rested the basket on the hood of a black sports car. "What are you having?"

"Some kind of casserole," he groaned, making it sound like a dirty word. "Chicken."

"With rice, vegetables and green chilies," Leah added, feeling silly about the need to defend her choice of entrée.

"Sounds good," said Ellen. "We're having macaroni and cheese out of a box. I'll bet Mr. Gorgeous Superhero will like your chicken better."

Leah hoped Mr. Gorgeous wasn't home, where he could hear the conversation from his window. It would be just her luck to have him listening to every word. Of course, her son knew every move the man made, so she might as well take advantage of the situation. "Will, is Jake home yet?"

"Nah. He's still at the church."

"Good." Leah opened the car door and motioned to Willie to climb inside.

"Well, good luck tonight," Ellen said. "Come on, Nan, I'll help you with the laundry and then we'll start studying like maniacs."

Leah rolled down the window and laughed. "Is that how it's done?"

Ellen grinned. "Sure. We're partying later on, though."

"Need anything at the store?"

"Tons," the girl answered. "But we're going to town later. Thanks, anyway."

Leah turned on the motor, watched Willie fasten his seat belt and carefully backed around the other cars before heading out of the driveway. Going to town for one item at the store was not her idea of organization and efficiency.

This was getting ridiculous. She'd been up since five to organize her day around a man coming for dinner. Not just a man, she grumbled to herself, but a damn cartoon character. Superman or Mr. Gorgeous or Kennedy Construction had better damn well appreciate this meal.

5

"THIS IS DELICIOUS," Jake said, forking another mound of rice. "What is it?"

"Just call it Pritchard's Corner casserole," Leah answered, pleased to see Jake demolishing her dinner. As far as she was concerned, the faster he ate, the faster the evening would be over.

Jake looked surprised. "Your own recipe?"

Leah nodded.

His eyebrows rose. "I wouldn't have figured you for the cooking type."

"The cooking type?" she echoed. "What on earth is that?"

Jake shrugged, realizing he'd put his foot in his mouth again. "Nothing, Leah. I would have thought you'd be too busy to come up with new recipes."

"I like to," she protested. "I don't have a lot of time these days, and cooking for the two of us gets pretty old."

He turned those gray eyes on her once again, and Leah braced herself for a personal question.

"What's in it?"

Willie answered, bored with the conversation. "Just stuff from the garden. You like that kind of stuff?"

"Sure. Why not?"

"Uh, I dunno." Willie looked trapped, and Leah masked her smile. *Score one point for Mom in the Vegetable War.*

"Thanks for bringing the wine," Leah said, after taking a

sip from one of her grandmother's wineglasses. "But you didn't have to."

"You're welcome," he said, toasting her silently with his glass. "And I wanted to. I appreciated Willie's invitation."

She didn't know what to say to that. He acted so happy to be joining them for dinner and she couldn't imagine why. "How's the church going, Jake? You said yesterday you were having trouble."

He smiled. "It's not going as quickly as I'd planned, but that's normal. I have to keep reminding myself that I'm not on a schedule."

"Do you have a, um, completion date yet?"

"Not necessarily. The quality of the work is the important thing. Anytime you want to take a look at it, come over and I'll give you another tour."

"Thanks. I might just do that."

"Me, too?" Willie piped up.

Jake nodded. "Yeah, but only when I'm around and you have your mother's permission."

Leah lifted the heavy spatter bowl. "Would you like more salad?" At Jake's nod she passed it to him, then said, "I know it's going to be a beautiful home." *If it's ever finished.*

"Thanks for the vote of confidence." He sounded as if he really meant it, and Leah felt a twinge of guilt. She supposed Jake could do anything he set his mind to. He certainly didn't lack confidence—he must have bushels of determination to take on such a project. She watched him add salad to his plate. "Have you had a chance to check those references and call my mother?"

"She wasn't home."

"Typical. Her sister lives nearby, so they're either shopping, playing bridge or trying to beat each other at tennis."

"Sounds like fun."

"It's helping her get over my father's death. They were very close." He paused. "What about the other references?" He'd carefully chosen people who wouldn't reveal who he was. His talkative and outgoing mother had strict instructions to follow, his banker knew nothing but how much money was in the bank account, and his cousin George—a reputable lawyer in Phoenix—specialized in discretion.

"All clear. I guess you're respectable enough."

"Despite your better judgement."

"Exactly." Leah wiped her mouth with the napkin.

"You should call my mother anyway," he said.

"Why?"

"She loves to talk on the phone."

"Then I'll keep trying."

"What about your family?"

"My father died when I was a baby, and I was raised by my mother and grandmother. It was a pretty quiet childhood."

"Sounds like it. You must have stirred up trouble somehow, though."

"No," Leah fibbed, thinking of her pregnancy. "No trouble at all."

Jake noticed there was no mention of Willie's father. Interesting, but not surprising. The woman kept her secrets well. "I don't believe it."

It was a good time to change the subject. "More bread?"

"Sure." He took the basket from her. "Thanks."

"You're welcome." Now she wished her son would say something. Anything. This conversation was becoming totally inane. Willie didn't let her down.

"What'd you do to get your bike taken away?"

It wasn't exactly what Leah had had in mind for a conversation-starter, but she wasn't going to complain. She looked at Jake, enjoying his pained expression, and waited to see if he'd answer the question this time.

"I don't think—"

"C'mon," Leah urged. "How bad can it be?"

"I really don't—"

"Did you kill something?" Willie's eyes grew wide.

Jake sighed. "No, I didn't kill anything."

"Were you six?"

Jake knew when he had lost. "Is this Twenty Questions again?"

"Yes, I guess so," Leah said. "Come on, confess. We're on the edge of our seats."

Jake put down his fork and rested an elbow on the table. "Okay, since you insist. I, uh, peed in a squirt gun and wreaked havoc and revenge on the gang of girls who'd broken into our fort."

"Peed in a squirt gun?"

"Wow!" Willie breathed, swallowing a chunk of zucchini.

"I was arrested," Jake added. "My mother fainted when the policeman came to the door. She thought I'd been hit by a car, but I was really hiding in the bushes in the backyard."

"You knew you were in trouble."

"Not until one of the guys heard that Mary Jo's mother called the police." He grimaced. "I guess Mrs. Kowalski had a strong sense of smell."

Leah wanted to laugh, but took a drink of wine instead. Then, after she felt she could talk, she said, "Well, that doesn't seem like something you should be arrested for. How old were you?"

"Ten. I went to juvenile court. The revenge against Mary Jo and her gang was classed as malicious mischief, and my cousin George and I had to do community service work."

Jake reached for the bottle of wine and refilled their glasses. "That was my one and only brush with the law. End of story."

"Your dad musta been really mad to take your bike away."

Almost the end of the story. The child really wanted to hear about having a father. Jake turned to Willie and shook his head. "He got mad because I scared my mother and made her faint right there in the living room. *She* got mad because George and I had been playing with the Bagdeluca brothers."

Intrigued, Leah leaned closer. "The Bagdeluca brothers? Who were they?"

"Twins. The meanest, toughest twins in New York, we figured. They lived one vacant lot away from Aunt Vivien, George's mother—"

"The one who lives in Florida near your mother now?"

Jake nodded. "And we weren't supposed to hang out with them, because every time we did we got into trouble."

"Did they, uh, contribute to the squirt gun ammunition?"

"No." Jake shook his head. "Their aim wasn't—never mind. My mother grounded me for hanging out with bad company, my father took away my bike for scaring my mother, and the judge made me and George mow the school yard for the rest of the summer."

"And the Bagdeluca brothers?"

"Moved away," Jake declared, picking up his fork and digging into his salad. "Not because of that," he added, anticipating the next question. "Their father was transferred to New Jersey. The neighborhood was never quite the same."

"Wow!" Willie exclaimed. "That's neat!"

Leah agreed with him, although she couldn't quite pic-

ture Jake as a ten-year-old kid, hanging out with two crim-
inals. They finished the meal in silence, Leah conscious of
the time ticking away, until a thought occurred to her.
"Don't you wonder whatever happened to them?"

"Who?"

"The kids in your neighborhood."

"Oh." Jake shrugged. "I know. George married and di-
vorced Mary Jo Kowalski. And the Bagdelucas are profes-
sional wrestlers."

Willie looked smug. "They never beat *you* up."

"No."

"I knew it."

Jake knew what the child was getting at. "They could
have if they wanted to," Jake started to argue, then gave
up. The kid would believe what he wanted to.

Later, as Willie cleared the dinner dishes from the table,
Jake saw Leah sneak a peak at her watch when she thought
he wasn't looking. Was the woman on a tight schedule on a
Saturday night? Probably. He'd caught a glimpse of the papers piled neatly on the desk in the living room, the books
stacked on the floor, and bright-colored folders stuck in
neat rows in some sort of metal holder next to the desk.
"How's school going?"

"Who are you asking about—me or Willie?"

"You."

"It's busy, but I love it."

He could tell by the way her eyes warmed when she
talked about it that she meant what she said. "So you rent
these houses, do word processing for hire and now go to
college full-time?"

Leah nodded, obviously uncomfortable talking about
herself. "That's right, except I don't do as much typing as I
used to. Just for a few of the neighbors and Paul."

"How?"

Her brow wrinkled. "What do you mean?"

"How do you manage to get it all done?" he asked patiently.

She looked as if she couldn't quite believe he was interested in the day-to-day details of her life. "Organization."

"The password of the nineties."

"The only way to survive without going crazy," she countered. "Would you like coffee and dessert now? It's brownies and ice cream."

"Don't forget the chocolate sauce!" Willie called.

"Sounds good to me," Jake said, "but let me help with the dishes first."

"No." She stood up and tossed her napkin onto the table. "I'll make the coffee now. It'll be decaf."

"Let me wash."

"No."

"Let me dry." He watched her efficient movements at the coffee maker and admired the cute little backside encased in black pants. "Let me help," he said once again. "Please."

"I'm only going to soak the dishes," she said, running the water into the sink. "I'll wash them later. You're the guest. Sit still and pretend you're sitting in the official dining room."

"I'm not a guest," he grumbled. "I'm a tenant and I'm sitting in the official kitchen, feeling ridiculous because you're waiting on me." Leah sighed, then tossed a dish towel in his direction. He caught it neatly and smiled. "My turn to dry?"

He stood too close to her as she did the dishes. She'd never washed so fast in all her life. Maybe he didn't mean to brush up against her—after all, it was a small kitchen and a microscopic working space—but for some reason she was overly sensitive whenever a denim-coated thigh touched her. He was too close, too helpful and too male.

Too much for her kitchen, that was for sure. At least there were only three sets of dishes—they hadn't had a party for fifty people— Leah didn't know if her nerves could take much more.

"Excuse me," she said, moving over to open the cupboard. "I need the dessert plates."

Jake took them from her, his height making it easy for him to lift the dishes from her hands and whisk them to the counter.

"Anything else?" he asked.

She shook her head. "You can sit down. The coffee's ready." The fragrant aroma filled the kitchen.

"Shall I pour?"

"No." Her teeth were almost gritted shut. "Just sit down."

"Where's the—Willie?"

"The bathroom." She took a brick of ice cream from the freezer. "I think he hides in there when there's work to do."

"Smart kid."

"Too smart, but then you know that." Now that Jake was safely out of touching range, Leah relaxed and started placing thick brownie squares in the middle of the plates.

"He's given me some moments," Jake admitted. "He still knows where I am and what I'm doing."

"He thinks you're going to slip up and leap over the church steeple in a single bound."

"He'll wait a long time." Then, after a moment's silence, "What is that?"

Leah turned around and looked at him. She lifted the plastic bottle of chocolate sauce. "This?"

He shook his head, looking at the three plates lined up on the counter. "Those."

Leah picked up two of them and deposited one on the table in front of Jake. "Brownies, chocolate chip ice cream and chocolate sauce. It's called mud pie in some parts of the country."

She sat down, sliding her dessert in front of her. "Go ahead, Jake. Try it."

"Mud pie," he repeated, reverence in his voice. Jake picked up his fork as he studied her from across the table. "Can we do this again tomorrow night?"

Leah laughed. "Absolutely not."

Jake lingered over a third cup of coffee—thankful it was decaffeinated or he'd be pacing the little cottage floor all night long—and had a second helping of mud pie. When he could drag the evening out no longer, he insisted upon helping his hostess clean up the rest of the kitchen. It bought more time. He knew Leah wanted to send him home so she could go back to her desk.

He said good-night to Willie, who was as reluctant to leave the kitchen as was Jake to leave the house. But the kid looked wiped out and practically staggered into his room down the hall.

Finally they were alone and Jake knew he had to go. Or get kicked out.

"Well," he began, standing up and easing toward the living room. "I guess it's time I went home."

He wished Leah didn't look so relieved. "Let me tuck Willie into bed first, then I'll—"

"Walk me home?" he teased.

"I was going to say I'd wrap up some brownies for your lunch tomorrow."

A few minutes later Jake leaned in the doorway and watched Leah toss brownies into a small, plastic bag. "If you start giving me leftovers I may get ideas."

She frowned and walked to the door. "Don't."

"My turn next."

"For what?"

"Giving you dinner."

Leah took a step back. "Look, Jake, I'm not really interested in—"

"Eating?"

"Dating."

"Neither am I," he lied. Or maybe it was the truth, after all. He suddenly wanted a lot more than just a date with the lovely Miss Lang.

"Good." She stepped forward, as if expecting he would back up and head for the front door.

Jake didn't move. He touched her shoulder and felt the warmth that lay beneath the thin fabric. "Tell you what," he drawled, looking down into those intriguing, hazel eyes of hers while he traced a trail along the side of her neck with his index finger. "As soon as I leave, you go over to that computer and type up a set of rules for us to follow. Things like No Dating, No Dinners, No Leftovers Unless It's Dessert, No Kissing."

"I get the idea," she whispered.

Jake touched her chin and tilted it slightly. "Good," he murmured, bending toward her mouth. "I'll post it on my bulletin board."

His lips softly brushed against hers. Something inside warned him to go slow when he really wanted to crush her to him, to pull her so close that he could feel her softness mold against him. *Go slow.* He did, dropping his hand to her shoulder while his lips sampled the warmth of hers. Jake increased the pressure, almost able to taste the tantalizing sweetness. He could feel her waiting, weighing whether or not she should let this happen. She trembled under his hands with what he hoped was passion, but suspected was fear.

A simple kiss, and she was worrying about it. He lifted his head and sighed. "Well?"

Leah didn't say anything for a second, surprise highlighting her eyes. The peach flush on her cheeks deepened as he stared down at her. "Well, what?"

"You're worrying about a simple good-night kiss."

"Was that what it was?"

"Yes," he lied. "And barely a kiss."

"Maybe that's how we do it in Pritchard's Corner."

"Next time," Jake promised, "I'll show you how we do it in New York."

"Uh-uh." Leah shoved the bag of brownies into his chest. "That's going to be against the rules."

"Whose rules?" He grinned, clasping the bag. "Yours or mine?"

"Ours."

"I can hardly wait." He winked at her and left the house. Leah listened until she heard his steps crunch on the gravel before turning off the outside light.

Damn. He must have felt her tremble. She hated that. He'd been driving her crazy and he knew it, too. He'd teased her with his lips, waiting to see if she'd fall into his arms for a passionate round of kissing and tongues and... *damn.*

A sex life was not on her list of priorities right now, although if she changed her mind, Jake wouldn't be a bad choice for a partner. He'd even be an excellent choice, she admitted.

Lust wasn't an option, either. Especially the unrequited kind that could keep a woman awake nights, wondering what the fulfilled nights would be like.

A college degree. She'd better reprogram her one-track mind. Right away. Leah went over to her desk and sat down, eyeing the blank computer screen with hatred. The psychology paper needed to be revised. It was due on Monday.

She already knew how they "did it" in New York. Without birth control, which had been her fault, too, but he'd said, "No problem," and she'd been naive enough to believe the withdrawal method really worked. That was why she had Willie—why she'd dropped out of college in her sophomore year, when her lover forgot she even existed and returned to New York to study pharmaceuticals. He probably sold condoms in his drugstore now. Leah hoped so. She hoped he dated women who insisted he wear them.

There'd been no need for birth control for the past six and a half years. Now there was need for an education, the kind that would not only support her son and herself but would enable her to fulfill her dream of becoming a psychotherapist. Finally.

There'd been no men in her life like Jake Kennedy, either, Leah sighed. He made her forget she had homework to do. Now *that* was what she called dangerous.

"PUMPKINS," Jake repeated. "You know, the big orange things you see at Halloween."

Leah looked at the calendar on her desk. "It's only October 13. Halloween is, um, eighteen days away."

"We want to get the pick of the crop," he countered.

"And my work is stacked up. I don't have the time to take the afternoon off and pick pumpkins."

"It's Sunday," he insisted. "A day of rest. A family day. A day to pick pumpkins, prepare for fall, bake an apple pie."

"I don't have time to bake a pie."

"I'll buy you one." Jake hadn't talked to her in over two weeks, hadn't been within touching distance in all that time. He'd tried to convince himself that his original idea of celibacy—at least until he'd finished the church project—was a good and valid plan. But he knew it was also hopeless. "Look, is there some sort of rule that states you can never take time off from your work?"

She almost smiled. "Yes."

"Then is there a rule," he asked, coming closer so he could see the gold flecks in her beautiful eyes, "that says you can't have fun?"

"No, but—"

"Then what's holding this up?"

"It's a package deal, you know. Willie and me."

"I know that," he said, exasperation creeping into his voice. "We'll take the kid, let him pick out a pumpkin, and then I'll show him how to carve it without slicing off his fingers."

"I'd appreciate that," she answered dryly.

"Good. It's settled." He frowned at the computer equipment. "Switch that stuff off—however you do it—and come with me."

She was only agreeing, Leah told herself, because she was sure she could make up the time later on tonight. Willie did look bored today, and he'd been good about giving her lots of time to work on weekends. Guilt edged its way into her decision to go with Jake. As a mother she hadn't been a whole lot of fun lately. Doing well in school was important to her. But the crisp, bright air beckoned and the sun was shining on this breezy, autumn afternoon. She pulled on a sweatshirt and felt just right.

Jake surveyed his landlady as she stepped outside five minutes later. Faded black jeans. Yellow sweatshirt, the color of a hot sun. Thick black socks and white sneakers. The woman looked good. Too good. Jake sighed and watched as she spoke into her son's ear. The boy ran into the house, the door banging shut behind him, and Leah approached the truck.

"Where'd he go?"

"To the bathroom," she explained.

"Does he want to get pumpkins?"

"Sure." She climbed into the truck, and Jake was irrationally pleased that she was going to sit close to him, instead of putting the small, wiggly boy in the middle.

"Watch the stick," he said, enjoying the brief contact of her calf against his leg.

"What is it?"

"For the four-wheel drive."

"I hope you're not disappointed. We don't get that much snow near the ocean," she said.

He grinned. "Rhode Island hasn't disappointed me yet." Jake handed her a folded section of the local paper. "Here's the ad I saw. Do you know where this place is?"

"Schartner Farm?" Leah looked at the map at the bottom of the ad. "I've seen the ads every year. I've always wanted to go there."

"You'll find a map of Rhode Island in the glove compartment. I still have trouble finding my way around sometimes."

"We won't need it." Leah helped Willie climb into the truck and fastened his seat belt for him. She gave Jake a few brief directions and they were on their way. The trip to Schartner Farm took longer than Leah thought it would, but southern Rhode Island's winding country roads looked their best in autumn colors, and Jake kept the conversation entertaining without becoming personal. To Leah's relief, Willie sat still. Aside from two questions about where they were going and how long it would be until they got there, he remained silent, clearly enthralled by the fact that he was riding in Jake's truck.

The pumpkins were a different matter. They lined the gravel paths and weathered wood porches, they were piled high on old wagons and lay sprawled in the acres of fields behind Schartner's store and greenhouses. Leah stood next to Jake, watching Willie examine eighty or ninety pumpkins.

"I hope you have patience," she murmured. "This could take a while."

It could take until Monday morning, Jake thought, looking down at the chestnut strands of hair brushing against his denim jacket. He was in no hurry. Leah stood closer to him than she ever had before, and Jake was content, even though he knew he partially blocked the cool wind.

"Come here," he said, throwing an arm around her and pulling her gently in front of him. "You're cold."

"Jake—"

"Shut up," he whispered in her ear. He placed strong hands on her shoulders as she stood in front of him. "I'm blocking the wind. Isn't that better?"

Leah nodded, although *better* wasn't the word she'd use to describe feeling Jake's large body behind hers. Bad enough that her shoulder blades grazed his hard chest, but her rear end snuggled against Jake's thighs. Lord knows what she'd feel if she dared move, so she tried to keep very still.

"Warmer?"

He rubbed her shoulders, and the warmth of his hands eased the October chill. She could have sworn he'd rested his chin on the top of her head for a moment. Leah tried to concentrate on why they were here in the first place. "Shouldn't you go pick out your own pumpkin?"

"I'm having a better time hugging you."

"We're not hugging."

His lips grazed her earlobe. "You're not. I am."

Leah shivered. *Damn the man.*

"Your ears are cold," Jake murmured, his tickling breath

sending a dangerous current of electricity along Leah's skin. "But your neck is warm."

Leah thought about moving away, but Jake was right. Her ears were cold. His body was warm. He was not playing fair. She decided to tell him that. "Jake—"

"I got the best one!" Willie called. He staggered from the field with an enormous, fat pumpkin cradled in his arms.

Jake moved to Leah's side, keeping an arm draped over her shoulder. "Are you sure it's big enough?" he teased.

"Yeah," the boy answered. "It's the biggest one in the whole field."

"Your turn," Jake said, motioning toward the piles of orange. "Everyone goes home with a pumpkin to carve."

Leah selected a smaller, pear-shaped pumpkin, while Jake, after much searching, discussion and deliberation, decided on a lumpy, odd-shaped pumpkin that defied description.

"But how are you going to carve it?"

Jake grinned. "I have power tools, remember?"

"To use on vegetables?"

"I'm only kidding. Wait and see. Maybe we should have a contest."

"Like the best pizza and best cheesecake."

Jake carried the pumpkins over to the scales. "Why not?"

"You're on."

Leah roamed through the greenhouses while Jake paid the salesclerk and with Willie's help took the pumpkins to the truck. She bought a large pot of bushy, white chrysanthemums, while Jake disappeared inside with Willie. When Leah caught up with them, they looked thrilled and Willie carried a white, square box.

"What is it?"

"Apple pie," Jake said. "I promised you wouldn't have to bake."

"Thank you."

"Want those flowers in the truck?"

She handed them to him, knowing it was useless to argue.

"Will you make me a cup of coffee when we get home?"

Leah couldn't help smiling up at him. He looked so hopeful. "Okay. I suppose you're bringing the pie."

"If you insist."

He took her elbow and guided her outside. "Come on, I saw about twenty women in there, ogling the dried-flower arrangements. I don't know if that's your idea of a good time, but after smelling those pies I can't wait any longer."

"You're used to instant gratification."

"You bet." He tossed his arm around her shoulders. "But when it's important I can be a very patient man."

6

IT WAS OBVIOUS from Jake's relaxed position on the living-room couch that he wasn't in any hurry to go home. Leah refilled Jake's coffee cup for the third time, wondering why she wasn't anxious to see him leave. Music played softly. He'd made himself at home, all right, finding her old Bruce Springsteen tapes and inserting one into the small stereo system.

"That's the last of the coffee," she said. "And there's one piece of pie left. You can take it home." She placed the cup on the coffee table.

Jake looked up from the photograph album. "You shouldn't wait on me."

"I wanted to empty the pot." Leah put the carafe onto the table and hesitated before joining Jake on the couch. She wished Willie hadn't dragged out the old pictures to show his hero. "You don't have to look at those."

"I want to." He flipped the page and studied a picture of the cottage. "The place hasn't changed."

"No. Everything's the same. Except Willie."

"Is he asleep?"

She nodded. "I just checked. Thanks for tucking him in. He was pretty tired."

Jake looked at his watch. "Eight o'clock. Guess I'd better get on my way and let you get to work."

"There's no hurry," she lied. Actually she had several hours of reading left to do, not counting polishing the psychology paper. But the temptation to relax on the couch with a friend—and look at her son's baby pictures at the same time—was too strong to resist.

"Cute kid," Jake said, pointing to a picture of a toddler trussed up in a blue snowsuit.

"Yes."

"What about his father? No pictures?"

"No father."

"Yeah, I guessed that."

"Then why'd you ask?" She tucked her legs beneath her, making sure she didn't touch Jake's thigh with her knees.

He leaned forward for his coffee, took a sip, then put the cup back onto the table before turning to Leah. "Just wanted to make sure."

"Why?"

Jake frowned. "I didn't mean to invade your privacy. I only wanted to know if there was a father behind the scenes." His gaze searched hers. "There's no man in your life, is there?"

"No." She lifted her chin. "And not necessary."

"I see that." He flipped to the next page of the album. "You take parenthood seriously."

"Of course. Don't you?"

"I don't have any kids. I've never been married, remember?"

Leah smiled. "Neither have I."

"Sorry." He looked embarrassed. "I didn't—"

She raised her hand. "Forget it, Jake. I'm not that sensitive, and besides, I feel very lucky to have my child. I've been able to support him, we have a home, and until a few years ago I had my grandmother's company. I was a lot luckier than most single mothers."

"How old were you?"

"Twenty. I'd started my second year of college and fell in love."

Jake shut the album and leaned forward to put it onto the table, then shifted on the couch to face Leah. "And?"

She lowered her voice. "He didn't know my name after I told him I was pregnant. He transferred back to school in New York."

"Too bad," he murmured. "And Willie?"

"Willie knows he doesn't have a father."

"What does that mean?"

Leah sighed. "He asked a couple of times why he didn't have a father, so I told him we didn't want to get married right then, because we had to go to school, and that his father lives far away now."

Jake frowned. "That must be hard on a kid."

"I wish I knew how to make it easier, but I don't. I've just tried to be honest."

"No wonder he wishes Superman would plop down in Pritchard's Corner and pay attention to him."

"This superhero stuff is getting on my nerves, but I try to think like a six-year-old."

"How does a six-year-old think?"

Leah ignored Jake's nearness. If she wanted to—which, of course she didn't—she could lean forward and rest her head on his wide, inviting, flannel-covered chest. She could close her eyes and just rest. "I've given up trying to figure it out. I'll let you know after I've become a therapist."

"Is that a joke?"

"No, that's a goal."

"A big one."

"One I've been waiting for for a long time."

"Good luck."

"Thanks. It's going to take quite a few years of hard

work, though." Leah gestured toward the stack of books on her desk. "Speaking of that, I guess I'd better get busy."

"Yeah, I guess so," he agreed, but made no move to leave. He tucked a loose strand of hair behind her ear. "That was a fun afternoon."

She nodded, thinking of Willie struggling to carry Rhode Island's largest pumpkin to the scale. "It was a good idea. Thanks for thinking of us."

"I had fun, too."

"I'm glad." Leah knew she should get off the couch, but didn't. Maybe he would stand up, wave goodbye, and let himself out the front door.

Jake's face drew closer. He reached over and slowly cupped the back of her neck, tugging her toward him. "This is another one of those good-night kisses you warned me about. I'm about to break the rules again," he murmured.

"I didn't print—"

He smothered her words with his lips as his mouth met hers. Hot and sweet, Leah decided. Coffee-flavored. Nerve-racking.

Nerve-melting, she amended, then ceased to think about descriptions as her body responded to his kiss. She didn't mean to reach up to twine her arms around his shoulders. She didn't mean to come to her knees as he pulled her against his hard chest.

She certainly didn't intend to tilt her head and slant her mouth along his in order to make kissing him back a little easier. He teased the seam of her lips with his tongue, and when she gasped for breath, he took advantage of the movement and claimed her mouth with skillful probing.

Nor did she expect to go so willingly into his lap when he stroked her sides with those big hands of his and lifted her onto him.

But against all better judgment Leah did. Her tongue danced with his, despite the warning signals exploding in her brain. She didn't want to stop, didn't want to pull her mouth away and leave his warmth. She liked his arms around her, and when his thumbs grazed the sides of her breasts, little shivers of need swept through her body, centering in an intimate, pulsing place.

"Jake," she whispered, pulling away slightly when he released her mouth.

"What?" he panted.

She realized she was on his lap, denim against denim, caressing the soft flannel shirt with the palms of her hands in a nervous motion. His hands stilled along her shoulder blades. "I think you'd better go home now."

"Why?"

"This isn't in my plan." She wished there was more conviction in her voice.

"What plan?" He nuzzled her neck.

"Stop," she whispered, pulling away, although she wanted to sink against his hard chest and start kissing him all over again. This was ridiculous. "I really don't have time for this sort of thing."

He looked into her eyes. "At this rate it's not going to take more than a few minutes."

Leah almost smiled at his wicked grin. "That's not funny."

"Yes, it is."

"All right, it's funny." She tried to slide away from him. "You're a real comedian, but I'm not interested in sex right now."

He eyed her swollen lips. "You're not?"

"I'm not," she repeated. "Look, I don't want to damage your fragile male ego or anything like that, but I don't have time for sex or making love or a secret affair or even just a friendly, one-night stand." She sighed, keeping her arms looped around his neck. "It's just too complicated."

"We could keep it simple." He grinned again. "Nothing fancy, you understand, just a few simple, basic—"

"Stop!" she groaned. "We both know I'm right."

"I don't want to get too personal," Jake began, "but since you're still sitting on my lap and we've been kissing for a few minutes, let me ask you one thing."

Leah tensed. "What?"

"Have you let any man near you since Willie's father?"

"No."

"Maybe that's the—"

Leah put her hand over his mouth. "Don't even think it," she warned. "Don't make snap generalizations. I'm not a man-hater because of one mistake. I'm not afraid to love again or anything like that."

"Then—" he mumbled.

"I've been *busy*," she said. "I've raised a child, held down a couple of jobs, and now I'm going back to school. I haven't had the time to make mad, passionate love to every available man who drove in the yard." She looked into the distance. "Not that any did."

With his free hand, Jake tugged Leah's hand off his mouth and kissed the soft palm. "I did."

"Yeah." She grinned ruefully. "And look where we are now."

He lifted her off his lap, setting her gently down on the couch beside him. "You're right," he declared. "Absolutely right."

"I am?"

"Neither one of us has time to get involved. I have a house to build, you have your studies."

"That's what I've been trying to say."

"Fine." He stood up and pulled her up to stand beside him. "Let's be friends."

Before she could move he cupped her face in his rough hands and kissed her. His warm lips claimed hers, while his tongue dipped along the soft folds of her mouth before she could protest. Not that she wanted to protest too much, she thought briefly, but if this was his idea of friendship, they'd be defining friendship in new and passionate ways on the living-room floor in about forty-five seconds.

She closed her eyes and decided to enjoy it.

When he finally pulled away, Leah knew she'd been thoroughly conned. "No fair," she complained, "we're supposed to be friends. What kind of a kiss was that?"

Jake touched her lips with his index finger as if to silence her. "Lady, that was a good-night kiss. As long as we're only going to be friends, I wanted something to remember you by."

"Well, you've got it. Good night."

"Good night. Tell Willie we'll carve those pumpkins in time for Halloween."

"I don't think there's any hurry."

"Yeah, but I promised."

Leah called to him as he turned his back and moved toward the door. "Jake?"

He turned around, hope in his expression. "What?"

"Don't forget your pie."

"WILLIE!" Leah looked around the yard. Willie was supposed to finish his after-school chores before going to town with her. This Friday afternoon was going to be full of grocery shopping and errands, as she had postponed the trip all week, trying to figure out how to make twenty-four hours a day seem like twice as much.

Only the chattering of a couple of blue jays answered her.

"William Lang!" she tried again. "Come home!" Leah began to feel nervous in the silence. He had told her he would be near the tree, and she hurried around the corner, hoping he was so enthralled with his action figures that he hadn't heard her call. The wind blew her words back into her face.

There was no reason to panic—yet. When there was no sight of a little boy anywhere, Leah made a quick trip around the property, stopping to knock on the farmhouse door. No answer.

Leah ran to Jake's, although his truck wasn't in the yard and hadn't been since early this morning. She knocked before daring to open the unlocked door.

"Willie?" she whispered, torn between hoping her son hadn't trespassed again and wanting him to be safe in the little cottage. The place was empty—not even a chicken disturbed the silence.

Leah hurried to the end of the driveway. Her only recourse was to check the church. Maybe Jake had let the child follow him, or maybe Willie—now that he wasn't grounded anymore—had chanced another spying expedition. He'd talked of Superman all week, and Leah had twice caught him watching the early-morning show.

The church area was quiet, and Leah wove through the piles of trash and lumber to the basement door. No one was around, since the carpenters' trucks were gone for the day. Leah looked at her watch, the panic turning her stomach into a queasy ball.

"Mom?"

Willie's voice was faint. She looked over to the pastures across the street. "Willie? Where are you?"

"Mom!" The voice was louder now.

"Where are you?" She hurried around the building. "Don't play hide-and-seek with me."

"I'm up here."

Leah looked up, following the maze of scaffolding toward the skyline. It climbed the building like some sort of weird fire escape. "Where?"

"Up here."

Her son was near the steeple, clinging to the outer corner of the tall spire like some sort of koala bear on the trunk of a tree. The top platform of the scaffolding looked as if it was only several inches below Willie's black high-tops. Leah's heart stopped, then started again at twice its usual beats per minute. "Willie, what are you doing?"

His voice was small and very high. "Climbing. I knew if I got stuck, Jake would help me."

"Jake's not here."

"He knows I'm in trouble."

Leah hurried to the base of the scaffolding and looked up once more. She would keep the boy talking, keep his mind off where he was. "No, he doesn't, Willie. He's not even home."

"He knows," her son insisted, but this time his voice trembled.

"Willie, don't move." *I will not cry*, she told herself. *I will not faint dead away on this pavement while my child clings to a steeple thirty feet up in the air.*

"I *can't* move," he answered. "I got scared. I cut my hand."

"I have to call the fire department." Leah looked toward the empty street. Where was a speeding car when you needed one? No one was around to make the call for her, and she hated to leave her son while she ran back to the house.

"Will they arrest me?"

"No."

"Where's Jake?"

"I don't know." Leah surveyed the scaffolding, noting the frames on the sides that could be used as a ladder. "Just don't move, Willie."

"I—I can't."

"I'll get you down." Leah, still dressed in the full denim skirt she'd worn to class that morning, reached for the hem and tucked it awkwardly into her waistband so the folds of fabric were high above her knees, freeing her legs for climbing. Then she rolled up the sleeves of the white blouse. "Hang on, honey. I'm coming up."

She debated kicking off her shoes, but decided against it. The moccasins' rubber soles shouldn't be any kind of hindrance and might keep her from slipping. She quickly climbed the first level of framework and continued. She kept looking up to see if Willie was still stuck to the steeple.

"Mom, what are you doin'?"

"I'm coming up."

"Mom, it's so high."

"Yep, you're right about that." She tried to think of what to say. "Don't look down."

"I can't," he called. "You're in the way."

"I'm coming to rescue you."

"You are?"

"Yes," she panted, pulling herself up on the metal bars. "That's the general idea."

"You're going to spank me."

A distinct possibility. "Oh, no," she fibbed. "I'm going to get you down from there, safe and sound, and then we're going to go to town and get a pizza."

"Pepperoni?"

Good, she was keeping his mind off the fact that he was clinging to a steeple. If she could keep him talking, he might calm down. Maybe they both would. "I'm getting mushrooms on my half," she said, concentrating on the metal bars. Her palms were sweating, and she paused to wipe one hand at a time on her skirt.

"I hate mushrooms."

Level three. "You don't have to eat them."

"Okay."

Leah rested for a moment, realizing she had another level to go before getting close to her son. She wished she'd thought this through more. Once she got up there, how did she think she was going to bring him down? All she could do would be to prevent him falling until someone—*please, God*—saw them and called the police. Two people hanging on to a steeple should be hard to miss. "How are you doing, honey?"

"Okay, I guess." The quiver in his voice made Leah climb faster, until she knelt on the ribbed metal floor at the top of the scaffolding.

"I'm right up here with you now," Leah tried to assure him. Luckily she wasn't afraid of heights, had repaired a number of roof shingles in her day and didn't feel the least bit dizzy when she stood up to touch her son. "Come on," she said, stretching up on tiptoe to grab his legs. "You're all right. I've got you now."

"I'm stuck," he whimpered.

"How?" She wanted to weep with relief when she felt his warm little body under her hands.

"The 'noculars. The strap." He started to cry.

"Okay." Leah kept her voice calm. "Hang on for a minute while I look."

Willie was indeed stuck, the strap of the binoculars hooked on a loose flap of roof shingle. To loosen it, he would have to let go of his grip on the steeple. That was too much, even for a six-year-old who didn't have the sense to stay on the ground where he belonged.

"Bend toward me," she said, then as he followed instructions without argument, Leah quickly released the strip of black plastic. "Now come down here. Slowly."

"O-okay."

One small foot inched toward the platform. Leah kept a grip on his legs as he moved. Once she got him onto the platform, she gripped his shoulders and hugged him.

"I'm in trouble, huh?" he sniffed.

Leah kept her arms tight around him. "Let's talk about that once we're back on the ground, okay?"

He nodded against her chest. "I guess."

"Good." She hugged him again, then released him. "What do you say? Do you want to rest, or do you want to climb down now?"

The little boy shuddered in her arms. Finally, after a long minute he said, "Go now."

"Okay." Leah sighed with relief. "I'm going to go first and you're going to be right above me."

After long, agonizing moments of inching down the ladderlike edge of the scaffolding, Leah and Willie stood on the comforting blacktop. Suddenly Leah crumpled onto the dirty parking lot and put her head between her knees.

"Mom? What's the matter?"

"Don't move," she said, her voice muffled by her skirt. "Just don't go anywhere."

"You want me to get Jake?"

"He's not home."

"Yeah, he is. I saw his truck when we were up high."

"Think he's going to fly over here?"

Willie scooted next to his mother and tried to peek through the copper curtain of hair. "You okay?"

"Sure."

"Then why don't you get up?"

Only a male would be so practical, Leah thought, her head still swimming. "I just don't feel like it."

"Are you sick?"

"My legs are tired."

She heard the crunching of gravel, then Jake's voice rumbled from across the parking area. "Leah?"

"Her legs are tired," Willie offered. "She's okay."

Jake didn't believe the six-year-old's diagnosis. "Leah? What's the matter?"

"I thought I was going to faint."

He crouched down next to her and caressed the back of her head. "Do you still think you are?"

She lifted her head and he caught a glimpse of her white face before she dropped her head back to her raised knees. "Yes."

"Are you hurt?" He looked at the length of exposed legs, wondering why she wore such a short skirt. She looked good, he decided, but this outfit wasn't her usual style.

"No."

"It's my fault." Willie tugged Jake's arm. "I thought you'd rescue me, like the boy in the movie."

"Like the boy in the movie?" Jake repeated blankly, studying the child's guilty expression.

"Yeah."

"Superman," Leah muttered. "The same old thing."

Jake felt lead settle in the middle of his gut. "Superman again?"

Willie nodded.

"And what was Superman supposed to rescue you from?" He braced himself for the answer. Whatever the kid had done had left his mother weak-kneed on the parking lot. "What'd you do this time?"

"Climbed up there." Willie pointed to the scaffolding.

Jake frowned, drawing his lips into a thin line. "How high?"

"I wanted to see the bell."

"The bell? The congregation took it with them to the new church. And besides, that's over thirty feet up—"

Leah held up her hand as if to halt his words. "Don't say any more, please," she groaned. "The spots were just beginning to fade."

"Sorry, hon." His hand stroked her back. He glared at Willie and the boy blinked back tears. "We'll talk about it later, after we get you home."

"Not yet," she said. "I think I'd just like to sit here for a while."

"It's going to rain."

"That's okay."

"Well," he said, "I think we'd better get your feet up."

"Why?"

"To get some blood back to your head," he said.

"Good idea," she muttered.

"How about if I carry you?"

"I don't think so."

"Why not?" He scooped her easily into his arms. "See? A piece of cake. And I can hold your legs up and your head down while I carry you back home."

Jake loved seeing her smile.

"IT'S ALL MY FAULT."

"No, Jake," Leah said, leaning forward at the kitchen table to rest her chin in her hands. "It's not. I haven't exactly been militant about my son's fantasy life."

"He's only a kid."

"And you're only the guy next door. You can't help it if some little boy has a huge imagination."

Oh, yes, I can. Jake shook his head. "No, I need to help the kid with this one." He stood up, scraping back his chair.

"I'll take care of it."

"The way you did today? Climbing up on the steeple to pull the boy down to safety?"

Leah grinned ruefully. "Superwoman would have done the same thing."

He didn't return the smile. "I'll talk to him."

"I spanked him."

Jake felt the guilt weigh heavier around his neck. "I wish you hadn't."

Her eyebrows rose. "I thought that's what you've been advising all along."

Jake moved away, leaving his coffee untouched on the kitchen table. "This is all my fault."

"Why do you keep saying that? It's ridiculous."

Jake shook his head. The time had come to tell Willie Lang exactly who Superman was: a has-been actor who lived next door. Make-believe wasn't reality. "I'm going to go talk to him, if you don't mind."

"Be my guest."

"Want me to get something for dinner?"

Leah shook her head. "I don't think I could eat anything right now, and if Willie gets hungry later I'll scramble some eggs." She picked up her glass. "I'm going to put some more brandy in this cup and then make some tea."

"Well, take it easy." Jake didn't argue. Half an hour ago she'd been white and shaking in his arms. Once he'd placed Leah on the couch and given her a cold cloth for her head, the color had begun to return to her cheeks. She'd described the climb up and down from the steeple in vivid terms—his imagination had filled in the rest.

Too bad a washcloth couldn't help him. Right now he had to confront a small boy who desperately needed a dose of reality.

"Will?" Jake stepped through the opened bedroom door.

"What?" He was curled up on his bed, facing the curtained window, but turned to look at Jake.

"Can I sit down?"

"Yeah, I guess so." He rolled over and scrunched his head against the pillow, making room for Jake.

"Thanks." Jake sat carefully on the bed, although the bright pattern of red-caped Superman figures on the bedspread did nothing to reduce his stress level. "We need to talk."

"Yeah?"

"Yeah." Jake took a deep breath. He was going to blow his cover, for sure, but he couldn't selfishly stand by and watch a little boy and his mother suffer because of Jake Kennedy's precious privacy. "What if I told you that I was an actor?" The boy's gaze never wavered from Jake's face. "A television actor."

"Television?"

Jake nodded. "Yeah. What if I was the *actor* who played Superman on the television show?"

Willie frowned. "An actor?"

"The shows aren't real," Jake said gently.

"Superman is."

Jake put his hand on Willie's shoulder. "No, he isn't. That's what I've been trying to tell you."

"You're just being mean."

"No, I'm not." Jake kept his patience. After all, he'd gotten the kid into this whole, idiotic mess. "That was my job in California a few years ago. I was hired to pretend I was Superman—Clark Kent, too—and the show was on TV for a few months before it was canceled."

"You're lyin'."

Great. Now the boy thought he was lying when he was telling the truth. It used to be the other way around. A no-win situation. "No, Willie, I'm not. I wanted to tell you, so you'd know that I can't rescue you from tall buildings or earthquakes or the bad guys." The child remained silent, staring at him with narrowed eyes, so Jake continued. "If I'd seen you on that steeple, I would have done the same thing your mom did—climb up and help you down or call the police for help."

"What about the double *L*?"

"The double *L*?"

Willie nodded, sniffling. "Paul told me that Superman only liked girls with names that started in *L*."

"Like Lois Lane."

"Yeah."

And Leah Lang, Jake thought ruefully.

"And my mom. And I have two *L*'s in William."

"Yes, you do, but I don't think that has anything to do with me."

"I don't believe you, Jake." Willie glared at him for a long second, then turned his back to face the window again.

"Okay." Jake sighed, patting the boy's stiff back. "Have it your way, kid."

When he returned to the living room, Jake heard Leah running water into the kitchen sink. He stood in the doorway of the kitchen and watched her for a long minute before saying good-night.

When she turned around, her face was still pale. "Going home?"

"I'm going to grab something to eat. Are you sure I can't bring something back for you?"

Her smile was shaky. "I think I'll stay away from solid foods."

"And the brandy?" he teased, hoping to keep her smiling.

Leah nodded. "And the brandy," she promised. "I think I'll just go to bed early."

Jake thought of tucking her in, then banished the provocative vision. He wanted to wrap her in his arms until she slept. He wanted to talk to her about Jeffrey Kent. But he knew this was no time to burden Leah with his honesty, so Jake simply left the house with Leah's soft good-night echoing in his head.

Later, in the quiet of his room, Jake sat in the dark on his single bed. Here he'd thought it had been a good month— no more supermarket gossip in the tabloids, and the season opener of *Fascination* had come and gone without his watching the show or even wanting to. He'd resisted the urge to read the Nielsen ratings in *USA Today*. But now he had to face up to the results of his actions. He'd thought he could pretend that Jeffrey Kent had never existed, but today's events proved that was impossible. Selfishly keeping the knowledge to himself could have cost a child's life.

Jake shuddered. What would have happened if Leah hadn't found her son in time? He needed to tell her who he was and to apologize for lying to her kid. It wouldn't be the end of the world if the residents of Pritchard's Corner knew he'd once been an actor. Most of them would never know who Jeffrey Kent was if they didn't watch *Fascination* or pick up a *TV Guide*. A Hollywood ego and his own inflated sense of importance had no place in his new life—his new life in Rhode Island with Leah Lang. *With Leah Lang?* An intriguing idea Jake realized and an appealing one but would the woman let him into her life?

Jake bent over to unlace his work boots. Damn. He could no more erase the mistakes from his past than Leah could, but suddenly Jake needed very much to try.

7

"ARE YOU AVOIDING ME?"

Leah paused in midstep, the mail she'd just collected from the box near the road clutched in one hand. "No. Of course not."

That was exactly what she'd been doing, and Jake knew it. He just dreaded discovering the reason behind it. He looked into those gorgeous, hazel eyes and felt his stomach knot up. The woman looked enticing even in faded blue jeans and a soft, white sweatshirt, and Jake wished he could spend the rest of the crisp, October afternoon indoors, making love to his wholesome landlady. "I haven't seen you for a week, not since the steeple rescue."

Leah winced. "Don't remind me."

"Any repercussions?"

"Not really, just a very quiet little boy. Are you looking for him? He's over at a friend's house until five."

Jake realized Willie hadn't discussed their conversation with his mother. He felt almost silly with relief. It was something he wanted to tell her himself, in just the right way. "You should have carved pumpkins with us yesterday. We had a good time."

"I heard all about it," she admitted, kicking fallen leaves as she started to walk slowly back to the house. "It sounded like fun."

Jake fell into step beside her. "We missed you."

"Wrong," she said with a chuckle.

"All right," he conceded, remembering Willie's contentment with the two-man project. "I'll amend that to '*I missed you.*'"

Leah didn't know how to answer. So what if he said he missed her? Was this another side to the Jake Kennedy charm? Flirting seemed as much a part of him as the tool belt he wore on his lean hips. She glanced sideways and saw that that particular contraption was missing today. "You're not working?"

"No, Leah." He sounded amused. "I'd go crazy if I spent every day working eighteen hours. It's Saturday afternoon and I want— I have other things to do."

When they reached her door, he opened it and followed her inside as if it were his home, too. She tossed the mail onto the pile of papers on her desk and turned around to face Jake, who was standing too close.

He looked over her shoulder to her desk. "Guess you're busy today."

"Yes." She sighed.

"Even on Saturday."

"Especially on Saturday."

His hands gripped her shoulders and he stepped even closer. "I've wanted to talk to you about something," he said, his voice low as he looked down at her. Her hair was loose, falling against his hands as they caressed her. She stood there patiently, as if she was only being polite. As if she wanted him to state his business so she could deal with him and get back to work.

"Anything to do with your cottage?"

"No." He decided he'd tell her about Jeffrey Kent some other time. Right now he wanted to take her mouth and explore the sweetness there. For at least three or four hours, before moving on to the rest of her delectable body. "Forget the landlady routine for a minute, will you?"

Her eyes twinkled as if she could read his mind. "Okay."

Jake didn't hesitate. The temptation was too great. Leah's lips parted, and when Jake pulled her soft body against his, he forgot everything he'd wanted to say. Her mouth tasted luscious, exactly as he remembered. Only this time he met with surprisingly little resistance from the woman in his arms.

It was the kind of kiss that left a man with no thoughts other than those of the warm, trembling woman in his arms, he decided when he finally lifted his head to look down at her. "Don't you think we can be more than friends?" he murmured, laughter in his voice.

Leah smiled at him. She liked kissing him, but wondered what she was getting herself into. Love took time. An affair meant an intrusion that would only complicate an already overwhelming schedule. "I doubt it." She caressed his cheek. "Although we do have our moments."

He looped his arms around her waist, keeping her warm body against his. "You never wrote up that list of rules for me to follow."

"I knew it would be a waste of time. I didn't think you were very good at following rules."

"Wise woman."

Leah nodded. "I'm glad I'm finally getting some respect."

Jake struggled to remember the reason he'd tracked her down. There was still a certain acting career to discuss. "You've recovered from last week?"

"We both had a few nightmares, but Willie's been very quiet and very good ever since. He hasn't talked about Superman at all. I'm trying to have a sense of humor about it now, but it's not easy."

"No, it isn't. Look," he began. "I tried to talk to Willie

about this Superman thing, but it wasn't very successful. I told him—"

The shrill jangle of the telephone interrupted his words.

"Excuse me." Leah reluctantly left Jake's embrace. She had to admit to herself that it was wonderful to be in his arms. Not the wisest place to be, but certainly tempting to stay. She straightened her sweatshirt, while hurrying into the kitchen to grab the phone on the third ring. "Hello?"

Jake moved to the doorway, shamelessly deciding to listen.

"Oh, sure. I remember." She paused after turning away from Jake's curious gaze. "Well, that's very nice of you, Mel, but—" She broke off, her cheeks turning rosy. "I just don't have the time to, um, go out with anyone right now, with work and classes, but thank you." Again a pause. "Sure." Her voice was warm. "You, too."

Jake watched Leah hang up the receiver. As she shot him a rueful smile, he asked, "Another admirer?"

"The doctor I met a few weeks ago. He calls every once in a while."

"And you give him the brush-off? Nice job."

"He's nice, but—"

"You prefer carpenters."

"I prefer peace and quiet."

"Liar." He walked over to her and kissed her lips briefly. "You prefer me."

Leah wanted to laugh, but his words were uncomfortably close to the truth. "Pretty sure of yourself, aren't you?"

"No," he said, his eyes twinkling. "I never expected to fall in love with a short—"

"I'm not short." *Fall in love?* How could he kid about something so serious?

He continued as if she hadn't interrupted. "Auburn-haired, college student-typist-landlady-mother and all-around-sexy lady."

Sexy? "Don't tease. You never know when I might take you seriously."

"The 'falling in love' part just might be true."

"And I'm Lois Lane."

"You're prettier than her."

"Jake!"

"I'm just stating the possibilities." He grinned as his large hands stroked the sides of her neck. "You're a great kisser. I could do worse."

"And what about me?"

He nodded toward the phone. "There's always Mel. You could do better."

She ignored his teasing. "Relationships take time, Jake. That's in pretty short supply around here."

"I'll take what I can get." His lips grazed her cheek and made a heated path to her earlobe.

Leah moved her head to avoid the provocative warmth of his lips. "Maybe that's what I'm afraid of."

"Make time for me, Leah."

"I just can't—"

"Ask me out."

"Ask you out?"

"Why not? I keep asking you, and most of the time you say no."

"Because I'm busy."

"Too busy for your friends?"

Leah thought for a second. Okay, if the guy wanted a night out, she'd give him one. "You're on. I'll ask you out—if you promise to go away and let me work until then."

"Until when?"

"Next Thursday."

He looked pleased beyond all reason. "It's a date."

Leah stood on tiptoe and kissed his cheek chastely before pointing to the door. "Bye, Jake. And don't worry—it'll be a night you won't forget."

"Now who's teasing?"

"Wear your work clothes. And your tool belt." She wondered how long it would take him to catch on.

"What?" He frowned, not moving.

"Do you have a hard hat?" she asked sweetly.

"Yeah, in the truck."

"Wear that, too. You'll look terrific." She watched as the significance of Thursday night dawned on him.

He grinned. "Halloween. I should have guessed."

"In the meantime I have work to do." Leah stepped past him and headed purposefully into the living room to her desk.

Jake went slowly to the door. "Well, hon, call me if you need someone to carve your pumpkin."

"IS THIS supposed to be your true personality?"

Leah adjusted her pointed, black hat and smoothed the full skirt of her witch costume. She ignored Jake's teasing, then purposely turned her widest smile on him. Her two front teeth were blacked out.

"Oh, Lord!" he groaned.

"Too glamorous for you, huh?"

"A woman with missing teeth and a purple mole on her nose?" He pretended to think it over. "I suppose I could overlook the faults."

"Sweet of you."

"Where's the kid?"

"I hired Paul to take him around the neighborhood to trick or treat. Stumbling around in this cold didn't sound like fun to anyone but a kid."

"I'd kiss you hello, but that green lipstick is a bit overwhelming."

It was foolish to feel disappointed, especially since she'd worked hard to look ugly. "Do I look scary?"

"Absolutely. I'm shaking in my boots." Jake thought she looked very cute, but he didn't want to disappoint her by telling her so. Her black-stockinged ankles and flat ballet shoes peeked alluringly below the shiny hem of her costume, and the brilliant chestnut hair tumbled from beneath the oversize hat onto a baggy, dark dress.

"I don't think you're afraid of anything, Jake. You're the most self-confident man I've ever met." She picked up a wooden bowl and held it out to him. "Want a treat?" He shook his head, and she looked him over from head to toe. "I like the red flannel shirt, and the down vest is a nice touch."

"It's to keep me from getting pneumonia. My coat's out in the truck. Do you know how cold it is tonight? And it's supposed to rain, which is supposed to turn into quite a storm before the weekend is over. Haven't you heard about Hurricane Lucy?"

"Sure I have." She smiled, showing the missing teeth once more. "If you're going to be cranky, you don't have to go out with me tonight, Jake. Willie and I can go to the party by ourselves."

"I'm not cranky," he said, putting his hands on his hips. He'd left the cumbersome tool belt at home on purpose. "And I'm not that easy to get rid of. What party?"

"An annual get-together down by the ocean at a friend's farm. A bunch of fathers make a spook walk in the fields every year. Tons of people go. It's fun."

"In the fields?"

Leah nodded. "Don't worry. I have a flashlight."

"Well, I hope you wear a warm coat over that witch

dress." Jake stepped closer to her and threw an arm around her shoulders in a casual hug. "Thanks for inviting me. How'd your week at school go?"

Leah blinked in surprise. No one asked her about school. Even Patsy, busy working full-time at the hospital, hadn't asked. "I got an A on my psychology paper."

"Hey," he said, looking genuinely pleased for her. "Congratulations. Do you have a lot of homework this weekend? I thought we could—"

Before Jake could finish, the front door burst open, and a small soldier dressed in camouflage green burst in. He rattled a bright orange bag. "Look at my stuff!"

Jake peered inside. "That's quite a haul." He was relieved, having half expected to see a miniature Superman, and hoped the military outfit signaled progress. Since last Friday, he and Willie had carved pumpkins, repaired the gate on the chicken coop and attended Paul's last football game—all without one word about superheroes passing between them.

"Why don't you leave it here now?" Leah suggested.

"I can't take it to the Pattersons?"

"You might lose it in the dark." At his disappointed look Leah relented. "Stick a few pieces of candy in your jacket pockets and leave the bag here. And don't forget your hat and gloves."

Willie shoved his hand into the bag and came out with a fistful of candy. "Here, Jake. I'll share. Want a stick of gum?"

"Can I save it until later?"

"Yeah." Willie loaded his pockets, ignoring his mother's wince. "Did you see the pumpkins, Jake? We put a candle in them."

"I sure did. They look great on the steps outside. I had mine in the window until I came over here."

Leah grabbed her coat, picked up a plastic-covered tray of cheese and crackers and stood by the door. "Come on, guys. It's almost eight."

"Yeah, Jake, this is the best part."

When they arrived at the farm, Leah realized Jake was right. The inky night was bitter cold and she was glad she'd brought her warmest coat. A skinny slice of moon hung above the wide fields while families lined up on the tractor path near the barn, waiting for the signal to start the trek to a distant pasture.

"I'll introduce you to everyone later, okay?" Leah whispered.

Jake took her gloved hand in his and gave it a reassuring squeeze. "Sure."

Willie ran off to join a crowd of boys climbing onto a nearby fence, but Leah decided she liked standing next to Jake's warmth. This was the first time she'd gone to one of the Pattersons' parties with a man beside her. She liked the feeling.

Jake's voice rumbled in the darkness. "Can you go out to dinner with me tomorrow night?"

"Oh, I can't. I have a lecture I have to attend." Leah hated turning him down again. She could get used to being one half of a couple, at least on an occasional weekend night.

"Saturday night, then." He looked down on her, a serious expression on his handsome face. "This could be your last chance, you know."

"Saturday night," she echoed, suddenly shy. It was one thing to be friends with Jake, but another to start officially dating. Why shouldn't she go out with a good friend? *Good friends don't kiss that way*, a voice inside reminded her. Mere male friends don't usually make you want to do a Susan Sarandon imitation and fall on your back onto the kitchen table, like in the movie *Bull Durham*. "Saturday would be perfect."

Jake kissed her briefly, and Leah felt a stab of warmth penetrate her cold skin. "Dinner, movie, you pick," he said. "All right?"

"Anything but pizza."

Jake nodded, his smile melting her all over again. "Ladies' choice."

The line of people began to move forward into the darkness around the barn and kids started screaming, making any further conversation impossible. Despite the chill, Leah laughed at the reactions of the children as scary monsters leaped around huge boulders, sending kids racing back to their mothers for comfort. The highlight was crawling through a tunnel of hay, where cold spaghetti hung overhead. But most of the children loved the entire show—until at the end, almost back at the house, the sound of a chain saw split the night.

Even adults screamed as the chain-saw man chased children around bales of hay.

"It's okay," Jake said, when he finally stopped laughing. "He doesn't have the chain on. It's just a lot of noise."

"Well," Leah replied, noticing that her usually intrepid son had drifted closer to Jake. "There's no blood anywhere, so I guess you're right. But the kids are still screaming."

Later, after retrieving the food from the car, she and Jake joined the crowd inside the warmth of the Pattersons' house. The adults, dressed in an array of costumes, gathered around the ten-foot island in the center of the enormous kitchen and helped themselves to the food, with the pot of steaming-hot chili on the stove as the main attraction.

Leah attempted to introduce Jake to as many people as she could in the crush around the island, but the noise made conversation difficult. She gave up and handed him a paper plate.

"There's a table full of desserts over there in the dining room," she told him.

One of the men handed Jake a beer, and he followed Leah through the crowd to where the hostess, Julia Patterson, dressed in a prairie bonnet and long calico dress, stood serving chili and handing out mugs of hot, buttered rum.

"Wasn't that a blast!" Julia exclaimed, picking up the ladle and dishing scoops of chili into plastic bowls for whoever wanted some. "The kids will never forget the man with the chain saw." She rolled her blue eyes. "I think it was Patsy's idea, which figures."

"Julia, I want you to meet the friend I told you about, Jake Kennedy."

Jake stepped forward. "It's nice to meet you, Julia."

She set the ladle down and turned away from the stove. Her smile was welcoming. "Hi, Jake. I'm glad you could join us tonight."

"Thanks for letting me tag along with Leah. I'm new here and haven't met many—"

"Jason Masters," Julia interrupted, a look of shock crossing her face.

"Who?" Leah inquired.

"You are, aren't you?" Julia, Leah knew, was always outspoken, insisting on nothing but the truth amongst her family and friends. "The voice is definitely Jason's."

Leah stared at her friend. "He's who?"

"Jason Masters." Julia's eyes grew wide as the realization sank in. "Or he's his brother. Or I'm making a big fool out of myself, in which case I'll recover."

"Well," Jake began, "you're not making a fool of yourself, Julia, but I'm not doing television anymore."

Leah listened, aware that she was being ignored. Jake put

his chili bowl onto the counter and took her hand, as if he was afraid she'd walk away and leave him.

Julia nodded. "You were burned to death in the stable. Did Sybil set the fire or did your stepbrother do it?"

Jake shrugged, keeping Leah next to him. "I don't know. The writers don't often let anybody know what they're going to do."

Julia turned to Leah. "Why didn't you tell me you had a star living next to you?"

"I didn't know." She tried to tug her hand away. A star? What on earth was going on here?

"I've tried to drop out of sight," he explained. "I'm not doing that show anymore."

"You're an actor?" Leah managed.

"Is he ever!" Julia said. "Some of the scenes he did with Sybil Cole were unbelievable, like that time on the boat when she took off her clothes—"

"Well," Jake interrupted, embarrassed. "That was a long time ago."

"What are you doing in Pritchard's Corner?" Julia asked. "You're living here?"

He nodded. "I've bought the old Baptist church and I'm remodeling it."

Julia grabbed her husband as he dumped another pile of paper napkins on to the island. "Harry, you're not going to believe this. You know *Fascination*?"

Harry winked at Leah. "That idiotic show you always watch?"

"That's the one—this is Jason Masters."

Harry didn't look impressed, just confused. "Aren't you the guy who knows the Bagdeluca Brothers? My son's a big wrestling fan," he explained. "I thought your name was Jake."

Jake put his hand out. "It is. I enjoyed the entertainment tonight."

Julia was clearly too excited to let Harry respond. "*Entertainment Tonight*! I remember when the whole cast was on for your final show. Didn't they have a cake shaped like the Harrington mansion?"

Jake nodded, and once again Leah tried to move away. So much for friendship with her new good-buddy tenant. Jake was some sort of sex symbol television actor, instead of a down-to-earth carpenter. These past weeks must have been very entertaining to him—charming the locals and all that. She didn't know why the fact upset her, but she knew she wanted to get away from him and fast. "I think I should go check on Willie."

"He's fine," Harry said. "He and Greg just grabbed a fistful of brownies and went back outside."

"Oh," Leah said. "Well, in that case, I think I'll get something to eat." She sipped her hot buttered rum and attempted once more to move away.

"I'll go with you," Jake said, squeezing her hand.

But Julia was still excited. "Pat, do you watch *Fascination*?"

Patsy Farrel, also a witch, but with a smaller hat and without green lips, looked up from arranging ham slices on an orange platter. "What?"

"*Fascination*. The TV show."

"Sure." Patsy looked blankly at Leah's face and back to Jake. "Hi, I'm Pat Farrel. I don't think we've met, but I know who you are. Are you going to give tours of the church when it's finished? You could sell tickets and make a fortune."

"I'd be glad to give you a tour anytime you want, but I have to warn you that it's a mess—"

"What's your stage name?" Leah asked, suddenly remembering the locked trunk that had so intrigued her son.

"Jeffrey Kent, but—"

Patsy interrupted. "That's where I saw you. I thought you looked familiar when you were in Leah's yard one evening. How do you like Pritchard's Corner?"

"I like it very much, but—"

"I guess you didn't want anyone to know who you were," Leah said, once again trying unsuccessfully to tug her hand out of Jake's grasp without calling attention to herself.

"Oh." Patsy brightened. "Do you wear sunglasses and funny hats to the grocery store?" Patsy was obviously in one of her teasing moods, Leah reflected.

Jake inwardly winced. The dark-haired woman's joking words were a little too close to the truth. "Sure. I've always tried to let Sybil have the publicity."

"She must really be something," Pat said.

"She sure is, but she's a good actress."

"You're a pretty good actor yourself," Leah murmured.

His hand tightened around hers. "Only on the soundstage."

"Could've fooled me," she replied under her breath.

Others had overheard the last part of the conversation and curiously began questioning Jake about Hollywood and his reasons for living in Rhode Island. Jake answered their questions with a matter-of-fact ease, and soon people were friendly without being awestruck. Even Julia seemed to recover from the shock of having handed Jason Masters a bowl of chili.

Jake knew a storm was brewing in Leah, though. He'd been forced to release her hand when she'd accepted a plate of food. Finally, when two tired toddlers burst into tears and someone said it had started to rain, Jake thanked his hosts and ushered Leah outside. It didn't take long to round up Willie, and ten minutes later Jake parked the truck in the yard. Leah had remained silent except for telling Willie he had to take a bath before he went to bed.

Jake followed Leah to the house and, once she'd unlocked the door, walked in without waiting for an invitation. Willie went right into the bathroom and Leah followed him to adjust the temperature of the bathwater. She didn't know whether or not she hoped Jake would stay.

When she came out, he was sitting on the couch and she sat down in the chair across from him.

"So have you a secret life," she said.

"Doesn't everyone?"

"Don't be cute, Jake. I suppose you're going to tell me that you're actually the guy on Channel 39."

"Superman."

"Yes."

He nodded. "I told Willie the day he climbed the steeple, but he didn't believe me."

"I feel like an idiot."

"Me, too," he said gently, "because I thought all along I had to protect my privacy. And it didn't matter at all. You have nice friends, who made me feel welcome both before and after the Jason Masters stuff."

"They're nice people."

"And so are you, and I'm sorry for deceiving you. I've tried to tell you several times—ever since the steeple climb—but something always interrupted."

"I wish it hadn't."

Jake stood and went over to her. "I'm sorry I'm famous." There was laughter in his voice as he bent over the chair. "Will you ever be able forgive me?"

"Not yet." Leah eyed him curiously. "So you're a sex symbol? Where does that leave me—the little lady you've attempted to charm so you could rent her cottage and share a few meals?"

"At first," he agreed.

"That's what I thought."

He put his hands over hers so she couldn't get out of the chair. "I said," he repeated, straining for patience, "at *first*. Damn, but you're a stubborn woman!"

"I'll take that as a compliment."

"Don't," he said. "At first you drove me crazy—you and the kid. But I'm being honest when I say I want to spend time with you. I've enjoyed our friendship, and I've honestly tried not to bother you, although I'm developing an enormous liking for busy college students."

"There are six next door."

"Maternal college students."

"Good night, Jake."

Jake refused to take the hint. "I'm asking you to accept me for who I am, warts and all."

"That's the trouble—you don't have any warts."

He chuckled. "You don't have to look so depressed about it. I can paint a few on, if you like." He reached up and rubbed the dot of purple makeup from her cheek. "Please, Leah. Don't let the past overwhelm a very enjoyable present." He frowned. "Be fair. All that *Fascination* business has no effect on my life in Pritchard's Corner, except that it's funded the purchase of the church and supports my restaurant addiction."

"I wish I could believe you."

"Believe this, then," he said, kissing her before she could protest. Leah couldn't resist kissing him back, but the warmth couldn't burn through all of her worries, and when he lifted his lips from hers, she took a deep breath and hoped he couldn't hear her heart pounding.

"I'll work on it," she offered shakily.

"Fine." He sighed, straightening up and backing a step away from where she sat. "Try to remember I'm just Jake Kennedy of Kennedy Construction."

"Who happens to have had a life of fame and fortune in Hollywood," she added.

Jake nodded. "I never asked you to apologize for your past, either."

With that he was gone. Leah shivered, although she still wore the wool cape. The wind howled around the house, and Leah went over to the thermostat and, refusing to think about her oil budget, carefully raised the temperature. The burner hummed on, and she could hear Willie singing in the bathtub.

All right, so what if the guy was no ordinary carpenter? Was it the end of the world?

Possibly, Leah decided, hugging the cape around her shoulders. Did this mean her home would be surrounded by television groupies? She could hear Oprah's enthusiastic announcement now: *Let's welcome...women who rent houses to sex symbols!*

She knew she should have trusted her first impressions.

Leah shivered again, and walked down the hall to the bathroom door. "Willie! Hurry up!"

"Coming!" he yelled, and she heard the bathwater draining.

Thank goodness. She'd tuck one very tired kid into bed and then take a hot shower. Leah refused to look at her overflowing desk top, deciding to crawl into bed as soon as she got out of the shower.

Halloween. It was a magic kind of night. Black magic. The mysterious Jake Kennedy had turned into a television sex symbol, right before her very eyes. Leah didn't know whether to laugh or cry.

8

SHE'D LAUGH, Leah decided the next morning as she made Willie a tuna-fish sandwich for his lunch. She'd apologize to Jake for taking the whole thing too seriously, go to her twelve o'clock class, then grab the necessities at the supermarket before Willie climbed off the school bus at three-thirty.

It didn't have to be the end of the world because Jake had once been an actor. He hadn't done anything too terrible or embarrassing since he'd moved next door. Just because he liked to have his own way, looked incredibly handsome, and behaved in a charming manner that made her look forward to seeing him didn't mean she had to join his fan club.

And just because he could kiss with bone-melting skill didn't mean she had to be susceptible to that particular talent. No matter who he was.

Leah tossed a small bag of chips, a granola bar and a carton of apple juice into Willie's plastic lunch box and set it on the floor in front of the door, so it wouldn't be forgotten.

"Greg asked me to stay over," Willie said through a mouthful of cereal. "Can I?"

"Tonight?"

He shrugged. "I dunno. Can I?"

"I'll talk to Julia, okay? Hurry up or you'll miss the bus. Have you brushed your teeth yet?"

He shook his head and scooped the last of the cereal into

his mouth before sliding out of his chair. Two minutes after Willie left the house, the phone rang.

"Great timing," Leah said when she heard who was on the other end of the line.

"I know what your problem is." Julia's voice was triumphant. "I've given it a lot of thought."

"Only one problem? Could you be more specific?"

"Very funny," Julia said. "I'm talking about Jason—Jake, I mean. I felt sorry for you last night, especially after I caught on that you didn't know who he was."

"Which is my problem," Leah stated.

"Not quite." Julia paused. "Leah, are you in love with the man?"

Leah gulped. "Julia—"

"Sorry, that's too personal. I've only known you since Lamaze class," Julia teased. "Don't answer it if you don't want to."

"I don't want to, but I'll bet you're going to tell me what my problem is anyway, right?" Leah sighed. She cradled the telephone receiver against her shoulder and refilled her coffee cup while waiting for Julia to elaborate.

"You're afraid," her friend declared flatly.

"Baloney," Leah answered, stretching the coiled cord so she could sit at the kitchen table. Through the window she could see Willie waiting with some of the other kids for the school bus to pick them up, sheltered from the rain by a kind neighbor's covered porch. "You'll have to do better than that."

"Aren't you the one taking the psychology classes?"

"Yes." She sipped the hot coffee and, remembering Jake's warning of a hurricane, wondered if she should listen to a weather report. "So far the professor hasn't covered the chapter on the stress of having television stars live next door."

"I don't mean you're afraid of men," Julia continued, clearly ignoring Leah's sarcasm. "I think you're afraid of falling for the wrong man again."

Leah thought of the dangerous gleam in Jake's gray eyes. "Well, you may have a point."

Julia's voice was strong with conviction. "I think you need more self-confidence."

"You've been watching Oprah again."

"Uh-uh. Sally Jessy Raphael. Tuesday was *Women Who Can't Make Decisions.*"

"That's not me," Leah protested. "Just because I don't have time to get involved with a man right now—"

"It's not about having enough time," Julia interrupted. "It's about having the confidence in your decisions when it comes to relationships."

Leah watched the school bus stop, lights flashing, then heard the gears grind as it started up again. "My last decision left me single and pregnant. So much for confidence."

"That's exactly what I'm talking about. You're afraid to trust your feelings."

"Right now I'm feeling like I'm going to be late for class," Leah fibbed, putting an end to the conversation.

"Okay, I get the hint. Greg wants to ask Willie to spend the night tomorrow. We're renting the wrestling show on pay-TV and he's invited a couple of boys over. Is that okay?"

"Sure. He'll be thrilled." Leah thought of her date with Jake and decided not to say anything about it. She didn't want Julia to think she had any more problems.

Twenty minutes later, just as Leah stepped out of the shower, she heard the phone ring and made a dash downstairs to answer it.

Patsy's cheerful voice rang through the receiver. "Hi, there!"

"Hi, Pat." Leah knew what was coming. She shifted the large bath towel around her, tucking the ends between her breasts.

"Tell me the truth. You really didn't know who he was when you met him?"

"No," Leah said, remembering the disgusted expression on Jake's face when he hauled Willie into the yard for trespassing. "I had no idea."

"He's crazy about you."

"That's nuts."

"I have a sixth sense about these things, Leah. Didn't I tell you about my sister Maggie?"

"The one who married Sam Somebody with the big house in Narragansett?" Little rivulets of water ran down her legs to puddle on the wood floor. Leah was glad the heat was on.

"Yep. Did I tell you they just adopted a baby boy?"

"Oh, that's really nice." Goose bumps dotted her arms.

"Well, before they were married, Maggie didn't believe me, either, but I knew something was going on and she kept denying it."

Leah's curiosity got the better of her. "How did you know?"

"It was that look in his eyes. Jake has the same intense expression when he looks at you. Possessive, like he'd murder anybody who stepped in between the two of you."

"He's an actor. He's supposed to know how to have looks like that."

"Yeah, well, sweetie, he's not acting now."

"Maybe you should be the therapist instead of me. You and Julia seem to know an awful lot."

"Did you see *Donahue* yesterday afternoon?"

"No. I missed it." Were both of her friends television addicts? "Who'd he have on?"

"Women who'd survived their man's midlife crisis."

"Not exactly relevant to my life, Patsy."

"How old do you think Jake is?"

"I don't have any idea. I have his mother's phone number, though. If I talk to her, I'll ask." Leah was only joking, but Patsy's silence made her wonder if her friend thought she was serious. "I'm only kidding," she added.

"I wished I'd taped it," Patsy muttered. "Maybe it's something you should see."

"Maybe I'll get to study the male midlife crisis next semester," Leah answered, hoping to make Patsy feel better. "Aren't you working today?"

"I'm going in late. I'll let you go—let me know if you want to go shopping anytime this weekend. Christmas is less than sixty days away."

Leah groaned as she hung up the telephone and heard the knock on the door. "Wait a minute," she called, peeking around the corner to the living room.

"It's only me," Jake called. "The sex symbol of the nineties."

She needed to round the corner and dash up the stairs to her bedroom. "Well, can you wait a minute?"

"The sex symbol of the nineties is standing out in the rain getting soaked."

"All right, all right," she grumbled. She went to the door and unlocked it. "Count to three," she said, "and then you can come in."

She heard his low voice call the numbers as she raced upstairs.

"Is this some sort of kinky New England game?" he yelled.

"I was on the phone," she hollered, "and I didn't have any clothes on."

"Fun game," he said, coming to the bottom of the stairs. "Can I play, too?"

Leah smiled, hurrying to towel off her damp body. She found the underwear she'd tossed onto the unmade bed and quickly tugged it on.

"How do you win?" he joked. "No, don't tell me. Let me guess."

The phone rang again. "Damn," Leah said, pulling a cream-colored sweater over her head before reaching for her jeans.

"Want me to get that?" Jake called.

"Please."

"Do I take my clothes off before or after I say hello?"

Leah zipped her jeans and hurried barefoot down the stairs in time to hear Jake's voice.

"Yes, she is." He paused, turning around to grin. "She's getting dressed. Hold on and I'll see if she can come to the phone."

Leah rolled her eyes. "Thanks," she hissed as he handed her the receiver. She'd never hear the end of this from whoever was on the other end of the line. "Hello?"

"Ms. Lang?"

"Yes, speaking."

"My name is Rhonda, from Penny Pincher Publications. We'd like to offer you a thirty-six-month subscription to your favorite magazines at a low, low—"

"I'm sorry, but I don't have time to read," Leah said, hating to hurt the woman's feelings. She hung up the phone, reassuring herself she had no trouble making decisions.

Jake's eyebrows raised. "Who was that?"

"Someone wanting to sell magazines."

"It's a good deal. I just ordered fifty-two issues of *Sports Illustrated*."

"Well, congratulations." Leah noted that Jake had tossed

his waterproof jacket over a kitchen chair. How long was he planning to stay?

"You can borrow them anytime you want."

"Thanks. I really appreciate the offer, but right now I'm trying to get to class."

"I thought you didn't have class until noon." He looked at his watch. "It's only ten of ten."

"How do you know when I have class?" She made a futile attempt to pull her wet hair away from her face, mentally cursing the telephone and wishing she'd had time to brush her hair and put on some makeup.

He stepped closer to her and touched a wet strand of hair, then traced an oddly thrilling path along her jaw. Leah couldn't move. "I've watched your coming and going for weeks," he murmured, bending his head closer to Leah's. "You really can stick to a schedule."

Leah thought about backing up, but the wall behind her barred a quick exit and she really didn't want to move away from Jake. Even if she should. "It's the only way I can get anything—"

Jake's warm lips cut off her words. His rough hands cupped her face to hold her still while he took her mouth. Leah felt the heat radiating from him and, against her better judgment, wanted to be closer. Her hands went around his waist, stroking the soft flannel of his shirt. She clutched the material as if that alone would keep him close if he wanted to pull away.

His tongue probed hers, and Leah felt her heart stop for a fraction of a second, then resume its heavy pounding. Jake tasted of coffee and mint and something sugary, and she loved the combination, loved the taste of him. Leah wondered fleetingly what his skin would feel like against her tongue, then banished the erotic vision from her mind.

He broke away, just long enough to slip his hands

around her waist and pull her against the hard length of his jeans before resuming the kiss. And Leah met him with a startling greed of her own. The rain pattered softly against the kitchen window, as if to remind them that it was much nicer inside than venturing out. A bellowing foghorn sounded a distant warning that mingled with the wind.

Leah couldn't think about going anywhere. Jake's hands slipped underneath her sweater and caressed her bare back as heat snaked through her body to settle where their jeans met. She wanted to rub against him like a cat begging for attention, but stopped herself. Asking for trouble would be a better description of what she'd be doing if she moved her body against the heat like a woman wanting to make love.

Jake lifted his head and looked into Leah's eyes.

The telephone rang again.

Leah leaned back and rested against the kitchen wall. There was no way she was going to answer the damn thing one more time this morning. She couldn't even breathe— how could she say hello and act normal?

Ring.

Jake paused. Leah met his gaze and slowly shook her head. If she'd had any voice she would have said, *Let it ring*, but she didn't need to. Jake got the message.

Ring.

His lips left a trail of heat along her neck, dipped into the chaste neckline of her sweater as his hands circled her back. Leah was glad she hadn't had time to put on a bra when she felt his thumbs graze the soft sides of her breasts. She gasped as his right hand moved forward and cupped her breast.

Slow hands. There was a song about that. Now she knew why. It had to have been written by a woman, Leah decided. Her body seemed to come to life under his fingers, and she didn't know how to stop it. Or even whether or not she wanted to.

Ring.

Jake lifted his head and looked into Leah's eyes.

"Three choices," he rasped.

"What?" She listened for the next ring, but the phone remained silent and she relaxed against the wall.

Without moving away, Jake lifted the receiver off the hook and set it on the counter.

"It's going to make strange noises," she said.

"Only for a few minutes." He turned his attention back to her. One hand still caressed her back, the other explored the round swell of her breast with gentle fingertips. "Your skin is so soft," he murmured.

"Jake..." She knew this couldn't continue. It would turn into something she wasn't sure she was ready for. Her body fought with her common sense.

"You have three choices for this morning," he repeated. "We can go outside in the cold rain to work."

"Or?"

"We can sit around the kitchen and drink too much coffee."

"Or?"

"We can make love."

He was hard against her stomach. Not even the heavy denim could hide his arousal. The heat wasn't her imagination, but he was giving her a choice.

"I choose making love," he said, his gray eyes dark and serious. "I would prefer to spend the rest of this miserable day worshiping your body." His smile was dry. "If that's not what you choose, this is the time to say so."

"I can't," she breathed.

"Can't choose or can't make love?"

Leah thought of her difficult Abnormal Behavior class at

noon. It was probably abnormal behavior to leave this man's arms, but she couldn't sacrifice her class. "Can't go upstairs."

The recorded voice of a telephone operator broke the heavy silence. "If you'd like to make a call, please hang up and try again. If you need help, dial O and an operator will assist you."

"I need help," Jake muttered, but laughter threaded his voice as a loud beeping burst from the telephone.

"I warned you," Leah said.

"No," he murmured, pulling her close against his body. His lips were warm against her ear. "I warned you."

"I have to leave in an hour," she protested.

"That's not nearly enough time." Jake sighed.

Leah wondered if he was kidding, and felt a stab of longing that was almost painful. She decided not to ask. "Want a cup of coffee instead?"

"Coffee's a poor substitute." But he smiled down at her before releasing her and arranging her sweater neatly over the waistband of her jeans. Once again he touched a strand of her still-damp hair. "You'd better go dry your hair," and he reached for the now silent telephone and replaced it on its hook. "I'll pour my own coffee."

"Thanks." Leah hurried out of the kitchen and to the stairs, hoping her legs would carry her up the thirteen steps. She knew she looked like a drowned rat, and her mirror confirmed it, although drowned rodents probably didn't have flushed cheeks or sparkling eyes.

Leah struggled to unravel some particularly stubborn snarls before she took a few minutes to wave the blow-drier around her head. At least, she thought, the beauty routine gave her time to catch her breath. She had to admit that her body was more than ready to make love with Jake. Her heart remained reluctant, while her brain was dead set against it.

"I was going to come over to see you this morning," she announced, when she joined Jake at the kitchen table.

He looked surprised. "Any special reason?"

"Last night. I acted like an idiot and I'm sorry."

"There's nothing for you to be sorry about, hon." Jake leaned back in his chair, the coffee forgotten on the table. "It's history."

"That's hard to believe. How could you spend so much time as a star and then give it all up to be an ordinary person?"

"There's something wrong with being an ordinary person?"

"You know I didn't mean it like that."

He smiled. "I know."

Leah thought of stopping by the local library for the back issues of *People Weekly*. Maybe she could find an article about Jeffrey Kent and *Fascination*. "I have to confess I've never seen the show. I've always taken classes on Thursday nights, but I remember hearing people talk about it."

"Have you decided where you'd like to go tomorrow night?" Jake grinned. "I'd invite you to my place, but it's a little small."

"Maybe somewhere expensive," she teased. "Now that I know you're rich and famous I should demand only the best."

"I'm not famous anymore. I've sunk into oblivion, which is just the way I like it."

"I don't get it. How can you give all that up?"

"Easy." He shrugged. "After my father died, I looked around at my life and didn't like what I saw. I wasn't very proud of myself."

"Why not?"

"I wasn't building anything solid. Just a career spouting someone else's words, pretending to be someone I wasn't, getting by on my looks and very questionable talents." He looked at her, his gray eyes dark. "Acting was an accident, something I fell into. I had no burning desire to be the next Olivier." He winced as if remembering, "Besides, standing in front of a camera wasn't what I wanted to do for the rest of my life. Haven't you ever felt like that?"

Leah studied Jake from across the table. He was warm and kind, a man she could care about. He was the sort of man a woman could depend on when the going got rough. She didn't think it was an act anymore. "Yes," she said finally, remembering her need to go to school, to finally complete her education. "I suppose I have."

He spread his hands out dramatically. "Then what's your problem?"

"I don't have one." *Love's a problem. Sex could be a problem. The fact that you're still in my kitchen could be a problem.*

He stood up and pushed his chair under the table. "I'd better get back to work." Leah didn't protest. Jake grabbed his jacket and tugged it on before walking out of the kitchen. He turned around, his smile turned down at the corners. "You think I'm suddenly going to leave my new house and head back to Hollywood, don't you?"

"I guess there's nothing stopping you."

Jake gave her a long, level look before answering. "Guess not."

LEAH DECIDED on the emerald silk blouse and matching skirt, purchased during a seventy-five-percent-off sale last spring, but finally had to face the fact that the pelting rain would only ruin it. She'd thought of stockings and pretty heels, though she knew the water sitting in puddles in the driveway would dip into her shoes and wet her feet. She hated having wet feet.

She hadn't seen Jake since he walked out of the house yesterday morning. There'd been a message, which Paul had relayed when she returned—rain-soaked, cold, tired and hungry—from Friday night's lecture.

"Wear something fancy. I'll be over at six-thirty," the note read. Something fancy. Easy for Mr. Television Sex Symbol to say.

The wind whipped around the house with surprising force, shooting the rain against the windows like pellets of sand. Leah hoped Willie was enjoying the wrestling party at Julia's and that the electricity wouldn't go off and ruin their fun. How on earth had her son grown up so quickly? An odd feeling of loneliness stabbed her.

Saturday night usually meant renting a movie—Willie's choice—and eating buttered popcorn. It was weird having a date. It was even stranger to look at her bed and remind herself she put clean sheets on it because she did it every Saturday like clockwork, along with the laundry and scrubbing the toilet. Why should smoothing crisp, floral sheets over the queen-size mattress suddenly taken on deeper significance?

Silly, she told herself. *They're only sheets. It doesn't illustrate any underlying sexual need to fall into the bed with Jake Kennedy.*

Yesterday morning hadn't been bad, though. The man certainly had the talent to turn up the heat. He was wonderful, and she had to admit that she liked him more than she'd ever dreamed possible. Love wasn't a word Leah used easily, especially referring to a man she'd only met a couple of months ago. Love was for families.

Leah turned back to her closet. What on earth was she going to wear? Discouraging was the word for it. Finally a chance to really dress up, and the dark, November night challenged her to look her best. It was a night for well-worn jeans, warm, thick socks and waterproof boots, plus a cozy sweater to top it all off. This wasn't a night for dresses and heels and spending time putting on eye makeup that the rain would only smear.

JAKE WAS five minutes late. Leah had decided on the only other dress she owned, a simple, black knit sheath. She wore opaque stockings, and black pumps so old even mud couldn't hurt them. If it did, she'd just toss them into the garbage. That is, she amended, fiddling uselessly in front of the downstairs mirror, if she didn't have a nervous break-down trying to drape this bronze print scarf around the dress's plain neckline. Leah wondered if she'd feel better grabbing a pair of scissors and slicing the silky rectangle into little pieces.

Thank goodness for her hair. It hung easily past her shoulders in waves, and Leah remembered the way Jake had touched her hair as he'd kissed her. Her stomach knotted and warmth flooded her body. If just thinking about him could bring on such a reaction, then what would she do if he touched her—melt right there, in front of everyone, at whatever fancy restaurant he'd chosen?

Leah removed the scarf, hoping to prevent the nervous breakdown, when a knock startled her away from the mirror. "Come in," she called, swallowing nervously.

Jake stepped inside. Drops of rain clung to his dark hair as he looked at Leah's dress and smiled. "Very nice."

"Thank you," she said. He shut the door.

"I'm glad you didn't change your mind." She looked soft and luscious, terribly sophisticated in black, heavy, gold earrings covering her earlobes. He wanted to take the ear-rings off and nudge her neck with his lips.

"Me, too." It came out in a whisper; she looked at the handsome man standing on her grandmother's braided rug. Jake wore a pale gray coat, a soft wool that looked like cashmere. He shrugged it off to reveal a charcoal suit, white shirt and deep maroon print silk tie. Totally gorgeous. "Did you need a winter coat like that in California?"

"I bought it in New York last Christmas," he answered. "You look wonderful." Jake stepped closer to her as if he wanted to take her into his arms. As if it was the natural thing to do. He stopped suddenly and looked around the living room. "Where's Willie?"

Leah stared at him, still stunned. She'd never seen Jake in anything but work shirts and jeans and fought the desire to step into his embrace and make certain he was still Jake and not Jason or Jeffrey of Hollywood fame. "He's spending the night with Julia's son, Greg."

He looked as if he didn't believe her. "We're all alone?"

"Uh-huh," she said with a nod. An almost intoxicating sense of freedom swept over her; she realized that the dark evening stretched endlessly ahead.

"Alone," he repeated. It sounded like a foreign word he needed to learn how to pronounce. He stepped closer.

"I'm, um, glad you like the dress." Leah knew he intended to kiss her and wanted to delay a few minutes more. Her resolve needed strengthening. She pretended his tie was crooked and touched the silky fabric with gentle fingertips.

"I like it when you touch me," he growled.

Leah looked up at him hesitantly, her palm still pressed against his tie. She felt the crisp shirt under her hand. So much for resolve.

"Maybe I have to make sure it's you." She smiled. "You look so different."

"Want me to change clothes?"

"No. You look terrific. I just need to get used to the new Jake."

"Same old Jake," he said, covering her hand with one of his and holding it against his chest. "No matter how I'm dressed, I'm the same man." *The same man who has fallen in love with you,* he wanted to say. Instead Jake ducked and briefly kissed her lips.

In love? The words echoing through his head stunned him, the implications of labeling his feelings for Leah took his breath away as he gazed into her doubtful expression. "See?" he asked, hoping he sounded more relaxed than he felt inside.

"See what?"

Had he ever been in love before he wondered, desperately trying to remember what Leah's question referred to. *Keep it light, Kennedy, or she might send you back into the rainstorm.* "Uh, I'm the same guy who uses any excuse to kiss his landlady."

"I've noticed," she murmured.

"Good." Jake wanted to crush her to him and feel her softness melt into his body. He'd walked around for two days fighting thoughts of Leah and the erection that accompanied them. He was hard again. If he brought her against him, she would feel how much he wanted her.

"We look pretty good, don't we?" she said, an impish smile on her heart-shaped face. "Where are we going tonight?"

Jake didn't want to leave the house. He looked down at the beautiful woman before him and put his hands upon her waist, tugging her close to him. "I'd planned on driving over to Newport, but in this storm I'd rather not."

"You're right." She thought of the bridges across Narragansett Bay that hopped between islands. It was not a night to venture across them.

He named two restaurants in Narragansett. "You choose whichever is better than the other."

"I've never been to either one."

"Don't you ever go out to dinner?"

"I'm too—"

"Busy," he finished for her. "I realize that." Jake kept her close. "But you've made an exception for me. Why?"

Leah stared up at him, wondering how she could explain it. She didn't dare tell him she'd never met a man who was so totally persistent and stubborn, yet considerate, too. A man whose smile made her want to run in the opposite direction, whose taste in food matched hers, whose kisses made her think she hated being alone at night. "I don't know," she said.

"Good. I like women confused and vulnerable."

"I hope you're kidding."

His hands tightened on her waist. "I don't feel like joking right now." Jake felt the tantalizing curve of her hips beneath the soft material of the black dress as his mouth met hers again. Her lips were warm, parting willingly, and Jake explored the sweetness waiting there. Waiting for him.

Leah moaned, a small sound in the back of her throat. Her hands crept up to his lapels. He trapped them there as he pressed one large palm against the small of her back and brought her against him.

"Do you feel what you do to me?" he groaned.

"Yes," she breathed.

Jake sighed, struggling for control. "We can't stand here much longer, Leah. Let's leave now, or we won't be able to."

"Are you hungry?"

His chest shook. "That's an opening line if I ever heard one."

"It's a simple question," she teased, struggling to ignore the delicious feelings spreading through her body.

"I'm hungry, all right," he rumbled. "And I have very exotic tastes."

"I'm not a very exotic person," she warned.

"I could argue with that," Jake said softly, nuzzling her neck. "You smell like tropical flowers." He lifted his head to study her face. "You're trembling."

"I know. I'm cold."

"Liar." His hands smoothed her hips. "You're on fire." The wind gusted noisily around the house, and the front window shook in protest.

He was right. Leah willed the thought of the clean, wide bed upstairs out of her mind. "You scare me, Jake."

"You think I've had tons of affairs and millions of hours of casual sex?"

"Yes," she whispered. "And I haven't. Just one man, one mistake—not exactly a great track record."

"We're not talking records here," he said patiently.

"I don't know. Maybe you experienced people should just stick together."

"I don't think that's quite how love works, hon."

"Are we talking about love?" She was almost afraid to hear his answer.

"And if we are?" He held her gaze with his own. "If I told you I loved you, had fallen totally in love with a woman who drinks champagne at eight o'clock in the morning and types her grocery lists—"

"How did you know that?"

He ignored the question. "If I told you I'd fallen in love, would it make a difference? Would it mean more?"

"I don't know. I don't really trust the words," Leah said.

"You don't trust a hell of a lot. It's the person behind the words, then?"

"Always."

"Well, at least we're on the right track." His mouth twisted into a smile. "Give me time. I'll grow on you."

We might as well be naked, Leah realized. She could feel the heat of him against her abdomen, even through the layers of clothing that prevented him from taking her standing up. She could feel his power, knew he wouldn't stop unless she asked him to. He'd given her choices yesterday, but tonight she was rapidly running out of time.

I want this man.

Her hands gripped his jacket, pulling him closer as his lips brushed her mouth and trailed along her throat.

Was this unavoidable? she wondered. Was there any reason to waste energy, trying to stop what was sure to happen next? What she *wanted* to happen next? The desire had been building since he'd kissed her and she'd ended up on his lap. She couldn't stop it. Tonight she didn't even want to.

Her hands went inside his jacket and brushed the warm expanse of cotton.

His hands slid to her buttocks and caressed them, pulling her even tighter against him.

"Three choices," Jake murmured against her lips.

Leah waited. She hoped her legs would continue to support her.

"Since we look so terrific, we can walk out of this house right now and have dinner."

"Or?"

"We make love in the living room—standing up, on the rug, couch, wherever—but it'll be hard and fast, if that's how you like it, because you're driving me crazy."

She wasn't thinking too clearly herself. "Or?"

"Or," Jake continued, lifting his head to look down at her. He didn't smile. His hands caressed her back, slipped up to her neck and tugged the zipper tab slightly. "We take it slow." The tab inched down. "We go upstairs," he said, his gaze on her face as the back of her dress slowly opened and the cool air kissed her bare skin. "I make love to you with my hands and lips and tongue until—"

Leah gasped as his hands slid inside the parted fabric of her dress and lower, to the ridge of lace rimming her hips.

"Jake," she pleaded, looking into his dark eyes.

His fingers stilled for a moment, and he took a deep breath before zipping up her dress. "All right." His voice was gruff. "We'd better leave."

Leah shook her head. "You haven't let me choose."

He raised his eyebrows. "I thought you just did."

"No." Leah smoothed her palms along the front of his shirt and slipped her fingers beneath the silky tie. Her fingertips traced tiny circles around the buttons as they explored the fabric.

"Touch one more button," he growled, "and I take you upstairs."

She could bear it no longer. There would be no turning back, no time for second thoughts. With trembling fingers Leah deliberately unfastened Jake's shirt.

9

HE SWEPT HER off her feet and into his arms.

"I wasn't finished!" Leah protested.

Jake smiled at her surprised expression. "I'm just beginning," he said, heading for the stairs.

"This is very dramatic."

"Yeah, I know. I've always wanted to do this in real life." He carried her easily up the stairs, pausing before entering the attic bedroom, waiting for his eyes to adjust to the darkness. The rain pounded against the roof, louder than it had been downstairs.

Jake stepped across the threshold and carried Leah to the bed. Centered against a long wall, it was a gray outline in the middle of the room. He sat her down on the edge of the mattress and knelt on the rug before her.

Leah reached for his jacket again, and this time he helped her pull it from his shoulders and she let it fall to the floor. She undid the knot of his tie with shaking fingers before finishing the job she'd started with his shirt, then smoothed her hands against the crinkly hair that covered Jake's warm chest. She couldn't believe she was actually getting to touch him; the freedom was intoxicating.

"My turn," he murmured. He took her hands away from his body and put them on the bed before slipping off her shoes and massaging the soles of her stockinged feet with light motions.

Leah suddenly felt shy. "I can undress myself."

"Not tonight." The mattress tipped her against his thigh as he joined her on the bed. "Turn around," he ordered gently.

When she obeyed, he unzipped the dress with careful fingers and slid his hands inside to caress her back. Tiny kisses thrilled her spine as his hands worked the dress off her shoulders to puddle around her waist. He swept her hair aside and Leah briefly felt his warm breath near her ear, then Jake's lips sent shocks against the sensitive nape of her neck.

"Jake," she whispered, needing to say his name in the darkness, needing to tell him how she felt as the crystal-clear realization hit her. But the words of love remained unspoken.

"I'll try to go slow," he promised, his voice a low growl against her nape. He lifted his weight from the bed, and turned toward her, holding out his hands. She twisted to face him. Jake took her hands and tugged her to her feet.

"Beautiful," he said, touching the swell of breasts above the lace-trimmed bra. "You're very, very beautiful."

Leah had never been comfortable with compliments. "It's also very, very dark," she insisted.

"Don't argue with me." He kissed her on the lips, unhooked the front clasp of her bra and drew it silkily down her bare arms. The cool air whispered across her breasts, but Jake's hands soon covered them with heated caresses. She gripped his waist in order to stand, because the heat radiating from him threatened to knock her over as if it were some sort of invisible force. As if it had a life of its own.

He trailed kisses along her throat and Leah's dress slipped past her hips to pool on the floor. Jake's exploring hands skimmed farther down, to the soft dip of her waist and lower, to smooth the suddenly sensitive skin covering her abdomen.

"I'm trying to go slow, hon," he groaned, lifting his head and gazing into her face. "But you're so beautiful, it's driving me crazy."

Did he mean it? she wondered. Leah's shyness began to disappear. "Come," she whispered, turning to tug the comforter back from the nest of pillows.

They sank into the bed together, Jake covering her with kisses as he explored her burning skin. She wanted him, needed to feel his bare skin against hers. Leah was on fire, the sweet, remembered pressure was building. She wanted to make love to this wonderful man who'd so quickly become part of her life. *Love,* she told herself, savoring the unfamiliar emotions. *Is this love?*

His clothing made a painful barrier; Leah tugged at the opened halves of his shirt, pushing the fabric past his finely muscled shoulders.

"Wait," he said. Jake slid off the bed. She heard his belt buckle hit the wooden floor along with the change from his pocket. When he returned, she felt the brush of warm skin as he joined her on the bed.

Jake lay on his side facing her, as if waiting for a word from her. When she was silent, he ran searching hands along her waist, to the curve of her satin-covered hip, then lower to the heated skin of her thigh. He stopped, hesitated, searched until he discovered the stockings. He looked down at her, surprise written in his expression. "A garter belt?"

Leah felt herself flush. "My grandmother never approved of panty hose. I guess I'm just, uh, old-fashioned."

"And terribly sexy," Jake murmured. His fingers brushed the sensitive skin of her inner thighs, causing Leah to suck in her breath. He would soon feel how much she wanted him.

But Jake's seeking fingertips explored no higher. Instead

they released her stockings. Kneeling, he slid them carefully off her legs before bending over to worship the delicate insides of her knees with kisses. Leah moved, wanting to reach for him in the darkness, but Jake held her legs still. He parted her legs with gentle pressure and caressed the silky skin of her thighs. He explored higher, his fingers brushing erotically against the moist, satin material between her legs, sending shocks of desire through Leah's body as he investigated the tantalizing combination of lace and skin before removing the scraps of fabric.

Jake knew where to touch, and his fingers worked magic.

He paused for protection, then moved his large body over Leah's in a nerve-shattering motion and claimed her mouth with his own.

"Now?" he asked, lifting his lips away from hers.

The satiny length of him slipped between her legs. Leah's throat closed. She nodded, unable to speak.

He eased her thighs farther apart to accommodate his size, and slowly entered.

Leah gasped.

He stopped. "Am I hurting you?"

She shook her head, realizing how big he was. "It's been a long time—oh!"

Jake moved deeper into her and braced his arms on either side of her head. He nudged the soft strands of chestnut hair aside with his lips, then nipped kisses along the side of her neck, waiting for her to become used to him. "Sorry, love. I don't want to hurt you."

"You're not," she said, growing more accustomed to the size of him as tremors radiated deliciously throughout her body. Incredulous with pleasure, she ran her hands along his lean hips and felt his strength.

Jake moved his hips slightly, rocking into her with a slow, thrilling intensity. His hard chest kept her a willing prisoner until he filled her completely. Jake made exquisite love to her, moving with fierce, possessive strokes until she exploded beneath him.

Leah couldn't stop the soft moan escaping her lips as she melted around him. He covered her lips with his own, her passionate whimpers dissolving against his mouth as endless, dizzying spasms took control. She felt him contract, expand, pounding heavy and hard until answering tremors shook his large body for long, powerful moments.

Leah heard the rain. The sounds of the world intruded little by little, bringing her back to reality. She opened her eyes. Jake slowly lifted his mouth from hers and eased himself away. He lay facing her with his head resting on the pillow beside her head. Their bodies, slippery with perspiration, still touched and the comforter lay in a heap near Jake's feet.

"Are you cold?"

"A little." She wondered if he would leave her now, hoping he wouldn't. "Are you?"

"Not yet." He smoothed a hand down her shoulder and lower, tracing delicate circles around a tight nipple with his index finger. He caught the soft swell of her breast in his palm and dipped his head to take the bud into his mouth.

Leah felt the remembered tingling. She couldn't get enough of this man. His touch excited her in ways she'd never known before.

"Mmm," he murmured, lifting his head to smile at her. "I'm hungry."

"For food?"

He nodded. "And other things."

"You owe me dinner," she teased, trying to ignore the sweet soreness between her legs. It was easier to tease than talk about what had just happened between them.

Jake dropped his head back onto the pillow and smiled at her. "Lady, you can have anything you want."

"I'M BURNING UP!" Jake could barely speak.

"I warned you about the hot peppers," she said, no sympathy in her voice. She pushed his water glass closer to him and watched as he grabbed it and drank thirstily. "You told me I could have anything I wanted."

"Within reason." He set his empty glass on the paper place mat. "I didn't expect to be tortured."

Leah looked at the Chinese fried dumplings on her plate and pierced a chunk with her fork, swirling it around the brown ginger sauce spiced with chilies. Her mouth watered.

"These are my very favorite things in the whole world," she admitted, popping it into her mouth.

"Leah, hon," Jake said, a strange look on his face.

She swallowed. "What?"

"Are you having an erotic reaction to Chinese food?"

She blushed. It was embarrassing, blushing at her age, but seeing the raw desire in his eyes brought back memories of the time they had just spent in each other's arms. "Sorry." Her voice was suddenly husky.

"Don't be." He carefully moved the chopped chili peppers over to the edge of his plate and doused the dumplings with extra ginger sauce before picking up his knife. "I love seeing that particular expression on your face."

Leah watched him, marveling at the easiness between them, remembering the hot shower they'd shared before changing into warm, casual clothes and heading out into the rain for hot food. "This has been an incredible evening."

"You sound as if it's over."

The restaurant was practically empty; smarter people

had obviously stayed home to watch television out of the raging storm. It was also after nine now, as they sat eating their appetizers before the main meal arrived. "It is."

"Uh-uh." He poured her more hot, Chinese green tea and then refilled his own cup. "This is only the intermission."

His warm, denim-coated knee nudged hers under the table. Leah instantly thought of the way he'd washed her body, lavishing soap upon her skin with his hands. She'd boldly returned the favor, memorizing the way he felt in her hands, stroking him into hardness. And, much later, there'd been the heart-stopping climax on the cold bathroom floor.

Leah inhaled shakily and picked up her tea. Her lips were a little bruised. She probably *looked* like a woman who'd been made love to for hours.

The slender Oriental teenager who'd taken their order returned with a tray of plates piled high and a large bowl of steamed rice. Jake rubbed Leah's knee with his and looked into her eyes for a long moment. Then he turned to the waitress. "I hate to bother you again, but would you put all this food in cartons, please? We're going to go home to... eat."

The girl nodded and added the plates of uneaten dumplings to the tray. "I'll be right back."

"Thank you," Jake said, never taking his gaze from Leah's face. "Do you mind?"

"No." Leah took her coat off the back of the chair and slipped into it. When the girl returned, she put a large brown bag upon the table and placed a piece of green paper in front of Jake. He pulled a generous number of bills from his wallet and left them on the table. Then he stood up, grabbing Leah's hand with one hand and the bag with the other, and together they headed out of the restaurant into the rainy night.

"You scare me to death," Jake said, shutting the truck door and handing Leah the bag. She cradled it on her lap after making sure her seat belt was fastened.

"Why?"

He took one hand off the steering wheel and grasped hers, pressing it between his legs. She felt the intriguing lump there and spread her fingers over the denim. "Maybe you'd better start the engine," she suggested.

The bag was hot against her lap.

"Feel me," he growled. "That's what you do to me. I've never left a restaurant like this in my life."

"It's the hot sauce," she teased. "Maybe you should stick to searching for Rhode Island's best pizza."

He put her hand back on the seat of the truck and stuck the key into the ignition. "I found the best pizza. I don't have to look anymore. Once I find what I want, I stick to it."

They weren't talking about pizza, Leah realized. "And cheesecake? Weren't you starting on a new quest for that?"

"Yeah," ne said, reversing the car. "I'm still searching."

"I'll make vou mine. It's a secret recipe."

"If you do," he warned, "I'm certain to fall in love."

Leah couldn't see the expression on his face in the darkness.

LEAH LAY QUIETLY in the bed, the morning sun glinting across the pillow in bright yellow streaks. Jake's warm body was pressed against hers; she was afraid to move, in case she disturbed him. Her rear end was tucked intimately against his abdomen and, if she wanted to, she could wiggle her toes against his furred legs. He snored softly near her ear, and Leah decided she liked the sound. It was definitely a luxury to have a contented, naked man tucked beside her in bed on a cold, bright, Sunday morning.

Too bad it couldn't last.

The storm was over. A brisk wind rattled the windows occasionally, the only sign that the stormy leftovers of a hurricane had whipped across the coastline and battered Rhode Island before heading north. The intrusion of cold, bright daylight contrasted sharply with the cozy, dark night that had blotted out the world. Leah didn't move, still afraid to wake Jake, afraid to discover that last night meant nothing to him. Or meant everything. She didn't know if she could handle either. Falling in love right now wasn't the most brilliant thing she'd ever done. It wasn't in her plan, had no connection to her life, and could only upset a carefully arranged schedule. A few years from now things would have been different, she knew. Why couldn't he have waited, come into her life when she had it all together?

Jake stirred, his breathing light and even. His arm came around her and softly cupped her breast. He inched closer to her, as if seeking her warmth. He kissed her neck, mumbling something she couldn't understand. When he stretched the tightening nipple between his fingertips, Leah felt the answering erotic pull. His scratchy chin rubbed her shoulder. She wanted to purr as his hand left her breast and dipped lower, to touch and probe her softness and press her against him.

Even just awaking, he remembered what was necessary. When he rolled back against her, Leah was grateful for the care he'd taken to protect them both. He slipped easily inside her, and it felt wonderful, despite the soreness from last night's lovemaking. He soothed her with his hands, twining his fingers through her damp curls and touching her with expert motions. As the delicious tension built,

Leah arched against him and felt the explosion deep inside. His hands stilled, and he held her tightly against him as he found his own release.

"Good morning," he said into her neck.

"Good morning," Leah answered. He was still inside her, and aftershocks still vibrated around him.

"You're wonderful." Jake kissed her shoulder.

Was she supposed to say thank-you? What was proper morning etiquette under these circumstances? She didn't want to leave the bed, but had no idea what time it was. The digital clock blinked, telling her the electricity must have gone off again during the night. She felt disoriented. If she got out of bed, she'd have to walk stark naked across the room to the bathroom. The cold, morning light became her sudden enemy, Jake's warm hands welcome chains.

She listened to his rhythmic breathing and realized he'd fallen asleep again. She moved and he slipped out of her. The man deserved to be worn out. She'd lost count of how many hours they'd made love. Slowly she eased away from him, relishing the privacy of these early-morning hours. Once out of bed, she replaced the pile of covers around him. Jake never moved. She looked at his handsome face for a minute, the brown stubble of beard making him look rakish and appealing. Leah sighed and tiptoed around the empty food cartons toward the bathroom.

She'd poured herself a third cup of coffee by the time he came downstairs after taking a shower. She'd wondered how long it would take him to smell the coffee and join her.

Jake stepped confidently into the kitchen and planted a kiss upon her mouth. "I made the bed," he said.

Just like a man, Leah thought. Did he think she wasn't going to change the sheets?

He opened the cupboard, took out a mug and poured

himself coffee. "I hope you don't mind. I found clean sheets in that little closet in the hall."

My mistake, she thought. *Visiting lovers must change their own sheets in California.*

He looked at her curiously as he sat down at the table and put his coffee cup in front of him, untouched. He looked fresh and clean and totally, devastatingly handsome. At least he looked more familiar in the jeans, even though the dress shirt was rolled up past his wrists and unbuttoned at the neck. "Is something wrong?"

Leah didn't know what to say or how to say it. She was in love with this man. It felt good. It felt awful. "I don't know."

Jake could feel her backing away from him. He knew he was losing her and wasn't sure how to stop it. He picked up his mug and warmed his hands on the hot china. "Last night," he began, searching for the words that would tell her what she meant to him.

But she stopped him, pain slashing across her face. "Jake, don't, okay?"

What on earth did she think he was going to say? "Leah, sweetheart, I—"

She stood up. "I made scrambled eggs. Do you want some?"

He joined her at the counter, twisting her around to face him. "I'd love anything," he said softly. "Anything that you have to give."

She looked as if she wanted to hit him with the rubber spatula. "Don't start, Jake. It's after ten, I have to pick up Willie at noon, and I've got work stacked up to the ceiling."

"I'm being dismissed."

"No." She regretted her impatience. "I'm being awful." She blinked back tears of exhaustion and conflicting emotions, feeling suddenly as if she was on a roller-coaster ride, going down.

"Come on," he said, smiling into her eyes. "Let's take a walk."

The wind from the ocean blew the breath right back down her throat, and Leah wrapped her scarf tighter around her face. She huddled in her down coat, thankful she'd worn something so warm. Jake pulled her to him by throwing his arm around her shoulders as they walked the path to Moonstone Beach. They weren't the only ones curious to see what damage the storm had done to the coastline.

A huge chunk of beach had been gouged away by the tide, so that a four-foot section of cliff dropped to a now narrow strip of beach. Leah took a deep breath. The sand was pale yellow, the sky a vivid blue, and the air cleared her head. They found a private area, partially away from the blast of the wind, and sat down on the damp, golden sand.

"Unbelievable what one night can do," Jake muttered.

Leah didn't know if he was talking about her bedroom or the storm. Either way he was right. She nodded.

"Want to go out for a Sunday dinner this afternoon?"

"I can't, Jake. I have to work." She waited, knowing there would be a battle.

Don't push, Kennedy, or she'll run like hell. "All right," he said, keeping his voice casual.

"You're going to have to give me some time, Jake."

"You have all the time in the world," he vowed. "No one's taking it away from you."

"Good." He heard the relief in her voice. "I just can't, I just don't—"

"What?"

"Have time for a relationship right now."

"You had time last night."

"Yes," she said, her voice soft. "And it was..."

Say it. "It was what?" He spoke in a careful monotone.

"I'm not sure what it was."

Jake put his arm around her and she huddled into his warmth. He knew he couldn't push. The lady needed time? He'd act like a damn cuckoo clock.

They watched the waves, their power greatly reduced, roll onto the shore.

HE'S USED TO the bright lights and big city. Pritchard's Corner would never be enough after its charm wore off, after the challenge of rebuilding the church wore off.

He's used to lots of women, lots of beautiful woman, adoring him. Leah had already figured out she could adore him a lot, too, but she was only one woman, one who had a lot of other things to do besides adore Jake all the time.

There were a million reasons why she shouldn't be falling in love with Jake Kennedy. Leah stared at the computer screen and thought of two more to add to her list.

He's never said he loved me, she typed. Actually, she hadn't given him much of a chance, though he had hinted at it a couple of times, she never wanted to hear it—until now.

He doesn't have much patience with Willie. Leah stared at the green print. Was that a fair statement? Maybe at first, during all that superhero stuff, but lately, well...the man certainly had the patience to carve pumpkins with a six-year-old boy. That was something. That was a lot. She pushed the Delete Line key, and the offending words disappeared.

Creating lists on her computer screen was typically ridiculous, and she knew it. She should be discussing these problems with the real-life man, not typing her worries into a machine.

But he had been strangely absent for the past four days, although Willie had seen him. She thought Jake was backing away to give her some space—at least, that was what she'd told herself on good days. On bad days she was convinced that he'd seduced her into a night of hot sex and now, having gotten what he wanted, he was moving on to new conquests.

She couldn't even type that fear into the computer, couldn't look at her silliness in print. After all, *she*'d unbuttoned his shirt. They'd both had a wonderful night. They were mature adults, who'd practiced safe sex and made no promises.

Sort of.

THE SCREAMING WOKE HER. She hadn't meant to fall asleep, especially at five-fifteen on a Thursday afternoon, during Oprah's show on people with multiple personalities. Although the future therapist in her was fascinated, the student was exhausted, and resting on the couch meant falling asleep.

Willie was screaming.

Disoriented, Leah jumped to her feet. She heard sobbing, raced to the front door, jerked it open and ran outside into the cold. Willie ran up the driveway toward her, his face streaked with tears. Leah's heart threatened to explode with fear when she saw the look on his face.

"Mommy!"

She grabbed him and held him by the shoulders, heedless of the chill surrounding them. "What's the matter? Are you hurt?"

Willie shivered, his eyes wide and frightened. "Robbers!" His eyes grew even wider. "Jake saw 'em and got hurt!"

"Where?" She knelt to his level. "At the church?"

"Yeah," he sobbed, falling into his mother's arms.

"Are you hurt, honey?"

"Uh-uh." He shook his head. "I got away from the truck."

"What truck?"

"The robbers."

"Are the robbers still there?" Leah knew she had to get Willie inside and call the police.

He shook his head. "Uh-uh. But Jake's got blood on him."

"Come on." Leah hauled him inside the house. She dialed 911 and gave them what little information she had, then directed Willie not to leave the house or unlock the door until she returned. She ran across the street, fear speeding her footsteps.

"Jake," she called. Darkness was descending quickly.

"Leah?"

"Jake," she breathed, running to where he lay near the corner of the building, beside the dark edge of the parking lot. "You're hurt."

He groaned in response. "Not really."

"But you're lying on—"

"I just don't think I can stand up."

Leah knelt near his head and touched the slippery nylon of his down vest. Blood. Her stomach tipped over, and she closed her eyes for a second, praying for strength.

"Go home and call the police," he said.

"I did that already. They should be here soon." Leah touched his face. "How bad is it?"

"Not bad." He tried to sit, but quickly gave up the attempt. "Willie and I drove over here to deliver some supplies for tomorrow. We walked right into a couple of guys stealing lumber."

Gently she stroked his hair away from his forehead. "In broad daylight?"

"Guess they figured no one would stop them. They looked like construction workers."

There was an ugly bump on his forehead. "How did you get hurt?"

"I told Willie to wait in the car while I checked out who these guys were, and one of them hit me with a two-by-four. The other had a knife."

"Hang on. Help's coming." She heard the police siren screaming from the nearby highway.

Later, when the excitement had died down and a paramedic had declared that Jake had a mild concussion, given him a tetanus shot and stitched up the gash in his arm, Jake lay on Leah's living-room couch. He was bare-chested, because the paramedic had removed his shirt to examine the wound. Leah tried not to look at the ugly bandage strapped around his upper arm when she came out of Willie's bedroom.

"How is he?" Jake asked.

"Asleep," she answered, joining him on the couch. "He finally stopping crying."

"I'm sorry, hon. When he wanted to come with me to the church and said you were asleep, I thought I'd be doing you a favor by taking him with me."

"It's all right," she said. "At least you're both alive. Willie will be okay. Tomorrow morning he'll think of it as a wild adventure to tell his friends in school. Come on," she put an arm around his shoulders. "You should be in bed, too."

He smiled. "Wish I had a fancy comeback."

"You're going upstairs," she continued smoothly. "You're not supposed to be alone. I'm to wake you up every couple of hours to make sure you're not unconscious."

Jake looked too tired to argue. Too tired to look pleased. "All right."

She helped him up the stairs. He disappeared into the bathroom for a few minutes, and when he came out he looked apologetically at Leah. "I don't have anything to wear to bed."

Leah wanted to laugh at his embarrassed expression. "Just take off your clothes and get into bed, Jake. It doesn't matter."

She left the room, taking her flannel nightgown into the bathroom to change. A few minutes later she looked like Grandma Moses, but felt warm and cozy and didn't care. She wasn't going to seduce a wounded man, after all.

"Cute," Jake murmured, gazing at her nightgown. "You'll match the sheets." He looked very comfortable, lying on his back, his head propped up on pillows. His bandaged arm poked out of the nest of covers. Leah turned off the light, pulled back the blankets and got in. Jake's body threw off an amazing amount of heat.

"Come here." He lifted the uninjured arm so she could snuggle into his shoulder.

"Does that hurt?"

"Everything hurts," he said. "I must be getting old."

His legs were bare. She contentedly snuggled up next to him and realized the rest of him was bare, too.

"I'd ravish you if I could move my head without seeing double."

"I'll take a rain check."

Jake pulled her closer. "It's been a long week, Leah. I've missed you."

"Me, too."

"I've been trying to give you some space."

"That's what I hoped."

He caressed her shoulder and she closed her eyes. "This is nice," he murmured.

"Um." She might as well accept the fact that she wanted to love Jake. Did love Jake. Would keep on loving Jake. Four hours of sleep last night finally caught up with her. The interrupted nap during Oprah hadn't helped much, after all. Tomorrow was Friday. Late class, she thought as she fell asleep.

Twice in the night, she woke up to check on him. He had stirred and she'd shushed him back to sleep. He took up a lot of space in the bed.

He kept her warm.

"ALL RIGHT, what's wrong?" Leah snapped the lid shut on the lunch box and faced her son. He hadn't said two words all morning, and now she worried that yesterday's robbery had caused more stress than she'd thought it would. "Jake's okay, you know," she assured him. "He's going to be as good as new."

"He was bleeding."

"I know." Leah inwardly shuddered.

"And he didn't stop the robbers and they tried to take his stuff."

"How could he stop robbers, for heaven's sake? It was two against one."

"He should of."

Leah recognized the belligerent gleam in her son's eyes. "Why?"

"He just *should* of."

"Because he's supposed to be Superman?" *Oh, please. Not that again.*

"Yeah."

"I thought we'd worked all that out. Jake talked to you about being an actor, didn't he? It was all pretend."

"I hate him." Willie picked up his lunch box and headed for the door.

Leah tried one more thing. "What about the, um, rock that destroys Superman's powers?"

"Kryptonite."

"Sure. Even Superman has hard times."

"That's bull, Mom."

It was worth a try. He started to open the door. "No kiss?"

Willie reluctantly turned around. He kissed her, and Leah buttoned the top button of his jacket. "It's cold out," she said. "You okay?"

Willie shrugged.

"Rough day yesterday, huh?" *Keep it light*, she told herself. *Don't get all dramatic over the danger he escaped yesterday afternoon.*

"Yeah, I guess."

"The police were real nice to you."

"Yeah. Can I go?"

"Sure. You need a hat?"

"Mom." He sighed. "Nobody wears hats."

"Okay." She touched his face. "See you after school. Maybe you and me and Jake will go out for pizza."

He shook his head. "No way."

"Willie—"

"He got hurt. He didn't do anything." He stormed out of the door. "I hate him!"

Leah didn't know what to say. She'd finally found a man to love—a man who was tucked neatly into her bed—and now her son didn't want anything to do with him.

The door slammed shut. There were some days when it just didn't pay to be a mother.

She swore under her breath.

"Leah, sweetheart, what else did you expect?"

Leah turned away from the window and the sight of Willie waiting at the bus stop with the other children as Jake entered the kitchen. He was naked except for a towel wrapped around his waist. "You heard?"

"Yeah." He came up to her and kissed her. "Don't look as if it's the end of the world. He'll get over it."

"But he says he hates you." She wrapped her arms around his waist and leaned against his bare chest for comfort. Leah decided she could stand here all day—this was definitely better than typing.

"And he'll get over it," Jake repeated.

"What did you mean—what else did I expect?"

Jake's chest rose and fell rhythmically under her cheek before he answered. "Leah, what about your father? I've never heard you mention him."

"He died when I was five."

"You've talked about your grandmother. What about other men in the family? Grandfathers? Uncles?"

"Jake—"

"Come on," he said tenderly, looking down at her. "Humor me."

"It was a small family. Just me, my mother and my grandmother."

"All women."

"So?"

"Don't you get it? All women, all living alone."

"I know," she agreed. "I have to do a paper on my family of origin, as far back as I can go. I've been dreading it, since it has to be about sixty pages long."

"Well, your family of origin is sadly lacking in men, don't you think?"

"We couldn't order them from the Sears catalog."

Jake didn't smile. "Willie did, sort of. He conjured up a hero right in his own neighborhood."

"His father didn't want to stick around to be a father, so it's now my fault he doesn't have any male role models?"

"No, hon, that's not what I'm saying. I'm just telling you that I don't blame the kid for being angry with me. His hero getting whacked in the head with a two-by-four wasn't written into the script."

"But—"

"He and I will work it out," Jake declared. "I've got a plan."

"You're a nice guy, Jake Kennedy."

"Yeah." He tugged her against him. "And you know what?"

Jake's terry-cloth towel couldn't disguise how much he wanted her. "What?"

His voice held a playful note. "I'm not seeing double anymore."

10

"I'M THANKFUL," Jake said, turning over in bed and murmuring into Leah's ear. "Very, very thankful."

"Why?" She didn't open her eyes.

"Thankful," he repeated, kissing her cheek, her nose, her lips. "That's the kind of day it is, remember?"

Leah still didn't open her eyes. "I have a sweet-potato casserole to bake."

"Shh." He moved his attention to her neck. "I'm busy right now."

"We have to get ready to go to the big football game this morning."

"Right."

"It's tradition," she said, feeling his hands evoke the familiar passion.

"Right."

"I promised Paul."

"Uh-huh," he agreed.

Leah moved toward him. She gave herself up to the delicious luxury of waking with Jake and opened her eyes. "Happy Thanksgiving."

Jake took her into his arms and pulled her on top of him. "That's exactly what I've been trying to say."

"SEE? We didn't miss the kickoff, after all," Jake pointed out. He kept a gentle hold on Leah's mittened hand as they entered the stadium.

Willie danced around them, amazed at the size of the college football field in front of him. "Can we sit anywhere we want?"

"As long it's on the side of South Kingstown," Leah said. "We're here to cheer for Paul, remember?"

She saw Paul's parents up in the bleachers and waved to them. It was a cold, clear morning, perfect weather for the annual rivalry between the neighboring high schools, South Kingstown and Narragansett. The stadium of the nearby University of Rhode Island campus was filled with spectators who made a tradition out of watching the teenagers play football each Thanksgiving.

She and Jake followed Willie up the concrete steps to sit beside Doug and Jeanne and Paul's younger brother. Leah introduced Jake, and the four of them exchanged polite conversation about the weather, Pritchard's Corner and the church renovation, while Willie searched for his favorite baby-sitter in the line of football players preparing for kick-off.

"Number seventy-four!" Willie shouted. "That's him!"

Leah, happily sandwiched between her two companions, snuggled into Jake for extra warmth, though she was wearing all the warm clothes she owned. She'd even forced a hat upon Willie and was relieved when he hadn't left it in the truck.

One little, happy family. Jake had been right—he and Willie were working it out, aided by the poster the Bagdelucas had sent, along with a personal letter to Willie with references to "our good buddy, Jake." They'd offered free tickets the next time the Wrestling Association tour brought them to the Civic Center in Providence.

"No problem," Jake had said when she'd asked how he contacted the brothers. "My mother keeps in touch with most of the universe."

Well, Leah decided, sitting with her thigh pressed cozily against Jake's, the universe was definitely operating on a smoother level.

It remained that way, from the football game—South Kingstown won—to the potluck gathering at the Pattersons' house. The crowd was in a festive mood, although several people questioned Jake about the robbery. He explained that the burglars hadn't been caught, and it didn't seem likely that they would be. The police had advised locking up everything carefully each night, and they had promised to put extra patrols on. Jake took some light teasing about his past stardom, but no one made an issue out of it. Even Julia treated him as just another one of the crowd, although she and Patsy both finagled invitations to see the renovations on the church. More people echoed their wish, and soon Jake agreed to give them all a guided tour after dinner.

There was a lot to be thankful for, Leah knew, raising her glass full of wine—Jake's undoubtedly expensive contribution—to Harry's toast to friendship and life's many blessings. Her kind friends. Her healthy child. And Jake, the loving man who filled her life with happiness.

Leah decided she must have drunk too much wine. She was feeling positively sentimental.

After an enormous dinner, they all pitched in to clear the table and load the dishwasher before piling into cars to see Jake's new home. Several older children were left in charge of the younger ones, so the adults could have half an hour to themselves.

Leah hadn't been inside the place in over two months, and when Jake unlocked the double doors and led the eager followers inside she was stunned. The walls were now covered with fresh Sheetrock, and the breathtaking sweep of windows framed a view of rapidly darkening fields. Jake patiently led everyone through the open living area, into the enormous, U-shaped kitchen and even upstairs to the master bedroom suite, accented by a magnificent skylight, and eventually downstairs to the old recreation room. Divided into what would be the bedrooms, the area was cleaner, but Jake's former room was still a jumble of dirt, boxes and piles of supplies and tools. Leah felt ridiculously relieved. He wouldn't be moving back to the church right away.

"Take your time locking up," Julia said gaily. "We're going ahead to put some coffee on and slice up the pies."

"Well?" Jake stopped at the door after letting the visitors out. He looked down at Leah. "What do you think?"

"It's all very...elegant." She didn't know what other word to use to describe what he'd done to the building. "It's hard to believe you've accomplished so much."

"Do you like it?"

"Of course," she answered. "Who wouldn't?"

The expression in his eyes was doubting, and Leah turned away. The classy, sophisticated home fitted Jake. Gorgeous and dramatic, yes. Maybe it would actually seem like a home when he installed carpet and furniture and decorations.

"The light on your answering machine is blinking."

He'd shoved his hands into the pockets of the soft, sable corduroy slacks, but extended one long arm and pushed the button to hear his messages.

"I'll go wait in the car," Leah began, but Jake caught her around the shoulders.

"Wait. This won't take long," he said. A man's nasal voice came through the machine loud and clear.

"Jake! Surprise, guy! This is Artie. You haven't returned my calls, so I'm flying into Boston tomorrow. Give me a call at the Westin, man, or I'll rent a car and track you down.

I've got an offer from the producers that you can't refuse."
A series of beeps indicated that the message was over and
there were no more on the tape.

"Artie?" Leah inquired, watching Jake reset the machine.

"Arthur Boxwell. My former manager and agent."

"He wants you to go back to L.A.?"

Jake shrugged, dropping his arm from Leah's shoulders
to reach into his pocket for the keys. "Maybe. Maybe not."

Fear clutched her heart, but she tried to look unconcerned. "Oh."

"You don't have to look as if I'm going to disappear into
the mist, never to be seen again."

Leah couldn't face his teasing. "I feel that way. You know
you can't turn your back on California forever."

"Why not?" His voice was calm.

"Because," she said lamely, "you just can't."

"Wrong, sweetheart." He grabbed her cold hand and
guided her toward the door. "I sure as hell can."

"Was it all that bad?"

"No," Jake said, looking surprised. "I just got tired of it."

He switched off a series of lights, then tested the lock, before stepping outside with Leah and shutting the door.
Leah felt the shock of cold air surround them. It was close
to sundown; a red line rimmed the horizon, and smoke
curled from the chimney of a nearby farm. Did he have a
short attention span? Was he the kind of man who would
grow bored and restless and want to move on?

"I'm ready for pie." He sounded cheerful again. "Didn't
Patsy say she made lemon meringue?"

"You have a one-track mind."

"I loved your sweet-potato casserole," he said, helping
her into the truck before closing the door.

She waited until he jumped in beside her and started the

engine. Welcome heat roared from the truck's vents. "Liar. I know where your mind is."

Jake grinned and laid his hand upon Leah's left knee. "It's not on dessert, sweetheart. That's for sure."

"Too bad," she said with a laugh, forgetting about managers named Artie and tempting offers at the Westin Hotel. "I made a cheesecake."

Evening descended quickly, and Julia made several pots of rich, black coffee before the crowd around the table had drunk its fill. There were more desserts than anyone could sample, a rich assortment of pies, cakes, sugar cookies and brownies.

"Remember," Jake said, helping himself to another slice of strawberry-coated cheesecake. "I told you I'd fall in love. I take cheesecake very seriously."

"Obviously." Leah watched the man demolish another thousand calories. Pat winked at Leah and she raised her eyebrows in response. She had no idea whether Jake was serious or not.

Julia refilled the coffee mugs. "Do you have any family, Jake?"

"Only my mother. She's with her sister's family in Arizona for the holiday," Jake replied. "I've been trying to get her to come north for a visit, but she says she'll wait until next summer. She doesn't like the cold much anymore."

"Me, neither," Patsy agreed. "I live for the beach."

"Not me," Jake said. "I'm waiting for snow."

Later, Jake helped Leah carry in the empty casserole dishes from the car.

"Take pity on me, Leah."

"Why?"

"I don't have a television set in the cottage, and the games are still on."

"You can stay." She looked at him, confused. "What makes you think you aren't invited?"

"That's why." Jake looked pointedly at Willie, who ignored him and went into his room.

"I thought it was getting better. Maybe he's just tired."

"True. I know I am."

"What about Artie and Boston?"

"I'll give him a call tomorrow."

Fine, Leah decided. If Jake wasn't the least bit excited or interested in what Artie had to say, then why should she be? Jake turned on the television and flicked the channel to the football game. In a minute Willie came out of his room, dressed in his sweatpants, lugging the pillow from his bed and one of his blankets. He climbed onto the couch beside Jake, fixed his temporary bed, and nestled contentedly against Jake's large, square shoulder.

Leah disappeared into the kitchen. There was no reason to interfere with male bonding.

JULIA SHIFTED her station wagon into Reverse and backed the car around. "We are crazy to do this, you know. It's the busiest shopping day of the year."

"Yep," Patsy agreed, apparently unconcerned. "But at least we'll get to go out for lunch."

"True." Leah twisted around so she could see Patsy in the back seat. "Think your daughter can handle that wild group of kids?"

Patsy nodded as they drove out of the Pattersons' driveway. "I've taught her well. They'll be fine."

"Everybody have a list?" Leah said.

Patsy groaned. "You're so organized."

"Tease all you want. I know you both have Christmas lists in here somewhere."

Julia nodded. "Mine's long. I'll never get through it today, but at least I'll get to start."

Leah couldn't believe she was going to spend a Friday at the stores. "This is decadent, heading to the malls like this."

"We're forty minutes away from bargains, shopping, lunch and freedom."

Leah agreed with Pat. It all sounded good.

"Yesterday was great. I think it was one of the best Thanksgivings we've ever had. Jake's wonderful, Leah," Julia said. "He doesn't act like an actor at all."

Leah thought of the way he'd swept her into his arms and carried her upstairs to bed. "Most of the time," she conceded.

"Well?" Patsy leaned forward to peer between her two friends. "Are you going to tell us it's serious, or what?"

"I don't know." Leah looked helplessly at the other women. "I just don't know."

"The church is great."

"Not homey, but great."

"True," Pat said, "but it has possibilities. Once you scatter a few hundred toys around, it might look comfortable. Where is he today?"

"Boston, I think. A friend, his manager actually, is there and wants to talk to him."

"Think he'll have to go back to California?"

"I don't think about it," Leah fibbed.

"You're in love with him," Pat stated. "Right?

"Yes."

"And he's crazy about you," Julia chimed in.

"He says he is, but I never can tell if he's just teasing or if he's really serious."

"He looks like he's serious."

"Well..." Leah looked out at the gray, overcast sky and

the line of bare trees on the edge of the road. "Sometimes it all seems a little too good to be true."

"Love's like that," Julia said softly. "Don't knock it."

IT WAS DARK—dinnertime—when Leah arrived home with Willie in tow. The trunk of the Subaru was filled with lumpy boxes that would remain hidden until it was time to wrap them. She'd splurged on sparkly silver foil, new, crisp, green tissue for the Santa gifts, and a ten-roll selection of shiny, multicolored ribbons. The urge to wrap presents grew stronger. How soon could she get Willie to bed, so she could pull out the loot?

It didn't take long to feed Willie, stick him into the tub and tuck him into bed. He'd played hard and long all day and looked relieved to be snuggled under his blankets.

Leah went outside to unload the trunk of the car. Jake's windows were still dark, his truck absent from its usual place in the driveway. Jake was clearly still not home, though she'd no idea what his plans were for the day, except to check with Artie in Boston.

Artie in Boston. She was starting to hate that phrase.

The whole area was quiet. The girls next door had gone home to their families for the long weekend out of school. After she carried everything into the living room, she switched on the television to keep her company. *Wheel of Fortune.* "How desperate am I?" she asked herself. Very desperate, she decided, leaving it on while a contestant with a Texas accent bought an *E.*

She tiptoed into Willie's room to make sure he was asleep. His breathing was heavy and even, his body snuggled deeply under the covers.

Safe. Leah hauled the giant wrestling ring from its Toy Superworld bag and looked at the pictures on the colorful box. Willie would love it. She'd splurged on wrestling figures, too. About ten inches high, they were modeled on famous wrestlers and were the right size to battle each other in the ring.

She'd treated herself to an inexpensive eye-shadow trio, a new package of high-cut underwear, and a practical turtleneck with padded shoulders. A cream color, it would go with almost everything she owned. Then she'd trotted through three of the best stores at two malls, searching in the mens' departments for something for Jake. It was tough, since she didn't know if he'd be around for the holidays or not. Maybe he had plans to visit his mother in Florida. Even so, you bought the man you loved a gift for Christmas. There was a rule about it somewhere.

Despite her best intentions, she hadn't found anything. It was actually sort of pathetic how few people she had to buy presents for. Something for Patsy and Julia, usually earrings or books, since they both loved jewelry and reading. She'd send Mr. Marcetti a little something, so he'd know they were thinking of him. Which left Paul—she usually gave him a gift certificate to the local music store.

Aside from Santa that was it. Christmas with no family seemed a little bleak, especially now that Willie was older. After tidily wrapping the wrestling toys, Leah hid the presents upstairs in the attic space, which was accessible only through her closet, then cleaned up the mess, so Willie wouldn't suspect anything. He still believed in Santa Claus, but this was probably the last year. Some wise guy at school would no doubt tip him off.

It grew later, the television programs failed to hold her interest, and every time she heard a car on the street she waited for headlights to beam into the driveway. She didn't feel like reading, even though she knew there were a lot of chapters left to study. Leah looked at her computer. She should get some work done on the "Family of Origin" paper.

Leah took a yellow, legal pad and a pen and went upstairs to bed. She'd get warm and comfortable and make notes for a while. She was really waiting for Jake, but didn't want to admit it. Jake had been up early, long before she'd gotten out of bed, presumably heading off to Boston. He'd kissed her goodbye and tiptoed away.

Leah yawned and looked at the clock. Ten-thirty. She wished he'd tiptoe back.

"COFFEE," Jake said softly.

Leah felt the bed sag when he sat down upon the mattress, but didn't open her eyes.

"Hi, honey, I'm home." His voice was threaded with laughter.

"What time is it?" She tried to open her eyes now.

"Eight-twenty," he answered. "And it's a beautiful day."

"That's nice."

He kissed her on the neck and she felt his warm lips tickle her lace collar. "I love your prim nightgowns," he murmured. "They're such a challenge."

"Go away," she mumbled. She remembered staying up late to work on her paper before crumpling against the pillows.

"Uh-uh. Willie's gathering eggs for breakfast, and I'm making it. You interested?"

Leah succeeded in opening her eyes and looked into his gray ones, seeing his handsome face, his gorgeous lips. "Yes, I'm very, very interested."

"Good."

"How was Boston?"

He shrugged. "It was a good meeting."

"Are you going back to California?"

Jake slid off the bed. "Not if I can help it."

Sweet relief flooded through her. "I'm glad."

"I don't take this lightly, Leah."

"This?"

"You and me."

She stayed silent, waiting. Then, "Neither do I."

Breakfast was great. Neither mentioned Artie or the offer that couldn't be refused.

"What are you doing today?"

"Working," she said. "I have a huge paper due in three weeks."

"Mind if Willie and I take off?"

Willie looked up from his third helping of bacon and grinned. "Where we goin'?"

"I have to pick out paint."

"Oh." The boy looked disappointed. "Then what?"

"I don't know. Go to the movies, maybe?"

"Sure!"

"I don't mind," Leah said. "I'm envious, but I don't mind."

"We could wait and go to the movies tonight, if you want."

"No. I'll love the quiet."

"That's what I thought. I'll pick up Chinese food on the way home, all right?" He lowered his voice. "I remember you like dumplings." His eyes twinkled at her.

"Don't forget the hot sauce."

SHE DIDN'T LOVE THE QUIET. She hated it. She wanted to be with Jake and Willie. Part of the family. She wanted to hold paint samples up to the light, go to the movies and eat popcorn in the dark of a movie theater. She wanted to hold hands with Jake.

Instead she worked, dipping into memories and research to examine her family's past.

A family terribly devoid of men, just as Jake had said. Was it warping her judgment? Did she think that somehow she didn't need a man in her life? Or did she just assume she didn't? Maybe she didn't even know anymore. Was she subconsciously pushing Jake out of her future, just because it wasn't part of her thinking to have a man around? After all, her grandmother and mother had survived on their own just fine. Why shouldn't—why couldn't—she?

She wanted Jake around.

She was going to tell him she liked having him around, just in case he didn't know it by now.

"CHRISTMAS," Jake announced, "is less than a month away."

Leah drank thirstily of her water, hoping to numb the bite of the chili peppers, so she could continue to eat the pork dumplings. "Uh-huh." She nodded.

"I have an idea," he began.

Leah waited.

"Let's go away for Christmas, somewhere up north, like Vermont."

"Vermont?" she echoed.

"Yeah. Vermont. Snow. A chalet. You, me, Willie and a Christmas tree."

"Hot buttered rum. Turkey dinner."

"Making love in front of the fireplace."

"Ice skating?"

"Teaching Willie to ski."

"Teaching me to ski."

"You don't know how?"

"No." It was tempting, so very, very tempting. Leah

rested her chin in her palm and looked at the man she loved. "When would we go?"

"Whenever school gets out. It will be my Christmas gift to you both."

"Willie's vacation starts December 20. I'm finished on the seventeenth. It's going to be hell until then."

"You look tired."

She smiled. "I always look this way."

"I know. Can you slow down?"

"Not if I want my degree. Not if I want to be a therapist someday."

"You'll make it." He touched her cheek with a loving caress. "We'll celebrate when you do."

"That's years and years away, Jake."

"I know." He looked serious. "We'll have a party. I'll take you to the Caribbean, so you can lie on a beach and get a tan."

Leah loved looking at him, especially when he was saying such intriguing things. "I'd like Chinese food at my party. Tables of it."

"Done."

"And I want to go to Bermuda."

"Why Bermuda?"

"Everybody I know has been there but me."

"Fine." He held her fingers with his own. "I will take the woman I love to Bermuda and feed her fresh fruit and drinks with rum."

"You should be careful about planning the future, Jake. Especially so far in advance."

"I'll take my chances." He frowned at her. "Aren't you the one who plans everything ahead of time? You seem like you have everything organized and well-ordered."

"Self-defense," she said softly. "If I organize, then maybe life won't get away from me and do something nasty."

"And what about love?"

"What about it?"

"You can't organize that, hon. It just happens."

"You can control your reaction to it. You can control how much you will let it affect your life."

"That's what you're doing to me, isn't it?"

"I'm trying," she admitted.

"Do you love me?"

She didn't want to talk about it, didn't want to risk saying the words, as if he could pick them out of the air, turn them into knives and cut her heart to shreds. "Yes." Honesty had always been her weak point.

"You don't have to look so depressed about it."

"Sorry."

"You don't trust me." It was not a question.

"Not really, but I'm working on it."

The fingers tightened around her hand. "That's a start."

JAKE DIDN'T WANT to tell her. His steps slowed as he approached Leah's front door. This was not going to be easy.

He knocked, the heavy, dull sound mirroring his feelings. Four days ago he'd talked her into Christmas in Vermont, and now he had to fly off to California for a week or two. It was unavoidable, but he hated it. Life, he decided, had too many complications.

"Come in," she called. He pushed open the door and smelled roast beef.

"Leah?"

"In the kitchen."

He rounded the corner. Her hair was pulled back off her face and her cheeks were flushed. Her hands were encased in bright yellow pot holders and held a metal baking pan.

"You're just in time," she said. "I've had this pot roast in the oven all day, so we could eat when I came home."

"It smells good," he said, stepping closer. He didn't kiss her, though he normally would have.

"You're welcome to stay," she offered. "There's plenty."

"I don't—"

"Jake!" Willie wheeled into the room. "Wanna see my new poster?"

"Sure, just a sec." He turned back to Leah. "Could we talk for a minute?"

Leah had set the pan down on top of the stove and shut the oven door with her knee. "What's wrong?"

"I just need to talk to you, but I can come back later."

The loud television, the anxious child and the obvious preoccupation of a woman cooking dinner didn't combine to make it a good time to talk about his trip to California.

"Fine," she said. "Where and when?"

"Eight o'clock. Come over?"

Leah nodded. "Sure."

He left after admiring Willie's picture of Hulk Hogan. He wished he could have stayed, but he had to pack. Maybe it wasn't such a bad idea to leave now as Leah was preoccupied with her schoolwork and upcoming tests. He'd be back long before Christmas, and she would have had time to get her work done without him around. He knew he was a distraction.

Once inside the tiny house, he turned on the lights and poured himself a glass of milk. A clause in his contract specified two brief appearances, if needed, during the following season, but the producers wanted him for three more episodes.

The money was tempting. It was a ridiculous amount for a week's work. The work would pay for both Leah's and Willie's college educations.

He was already thinking like a husband and father. Jake

laughed at himself and made a peanut butter and jelly sandwich.

LEAH REALIZED she should never have invited Jake to stay for dinner. It was too cozy, too "happy homemaker," too much of the "way to a man's heart" sort of trap. No wonder he'd practically bolted.

She hadn't meant it to be, but could see how it looked. All that was missing was the gingham apron and the home-made rolls. Leah looked guiltily at the frozen supermarket ones in their plastic bag. No one would ever have known she hadn't made them herself. Did Jake think she was getting too many domestic ideas?

A person had to cook because she—and her son—had to eat. Could she help it if she liked to cook? Could she help it if she was organized enough on a very busy Tuesday to stick dinner into a low oven and let it take care of itself all day?

Damn. She wished he'd stayed and told her what was wrong.

THE AIR WAS COLD, rich with the heavy scent of impending snow. No stars sparkled through the overcast sky as Leah hurried across the frozen grass to Jake's cottage. She only knocked once.

"Hi," she said, stepping into the tight, warm room.

He turned around from making his bed, tossing the tangled blanket onto the mattress. "Sorry about the mess."

A puffy, leather bag lay unzipped on the floor, and Leah stared at it for a long moment. Maybe he planned to move into his new home. "Going somewhere?"

"That's what I wanted to talk to you about."

It didn't take a genius to put two and two together. "California?"

He nodded. "Yeah."

"Stardom calls," she said wryly. "Artie's offer?"

"Not exactly." He stepped over to her and put his hands upon her shoulders, but the familiar warmth did little to make her feel better. "It's a little problem with my contract."

"And?"

"I'm going to have to meet with the producers in person and see what it's going to take to iron this out." He was afraid to tell her about his very possible reappearance on *Fascination*.

"Why? Can't Artie do it?"

"No," he said, his gray eyes somber as he looked at her. "I have to do it myself."

"Well, have a good trip." Leah knew it was ridiculous to feel so awful about him leaving for a while, but it was as if she'd just gotten hit in the gut with a lead basketball.

"I'm coming back," he reassured her. "Christmas in Vermont, remember? I've already made the reservations. You should be getting something in the mail soon."

"Sure."

"Think how much peace and quiet you'll have without me around. You'll get all your homework done."

"Sure."

Jake kissed her, putting all the heat, passion and promise he could into the kiss. "I won't be gone long," he said again. "How could I stay away from you for long?"

"I don't know. How?"

"I don't know either. I wish you could come with me."

"No way."

"I knew you'd say that, so I didn't bother to ask."

"Right." That would be real cute. The country girlfriend, hobnobbing with Sybil Cole and the rest of the *Fascination* cast. They probably could use some therapy, though. She could test out some of the theories she'd learned, she thought wryly. "I have studying to do, so I'd better get back. What time are you leaving?"

"Early. I'm catching a seven o'clock flight to New York, then on to L.A."

"Need a ride to the airport? I don't mind getting up early."

"No, hon, but thanks. I'll leave my truck, because I don't know how long I'll have to be there."

"Oh." This was serious. No, of course it wasn't. "I'll miss you," she said, tugging him to her.

Their lips met, and it was a long moment later when they separated. Leah opened the door. "You fixed it."

"Yeah."

"Great."

"I'll call you from L.A."

"I'd like that."

"I'll miss you."

"I love you."

"I love you, too."

That was the ridiculous part of all this, Leah decided later on, when she snuggled into her lonely, cold bed. She did love him. Was she an idiot to love a guy who could leave so easily?

No, because everybody and anybody could leave the person they loved.

Love wasn't a chain, wasn't an everlasting promise never to be broken. It died all the time.

There was nothing she could do except get her studying done, plan for Christmas. She wouldn't have any trouble keeping busy. She might even get more work done without Jake around. Maybe Julia or Pat would like to go shopping again. She could take a poll of the husbands and see what they wanted for Christmas. Maybe she'd get some good ideas for Jake's gift, too.

Leah pulled the blankets tighter around her. She would act as though nothing at all was wrong. Everybody went away on business—maybe this *was* merely a business trip, not the end of a love affair.

11

"THIS IS GOING to take longer than I thought." Jake sounded far away. The long-distance crackle coated his words, but Leah got the message loud and clear: the man didn't want to come back. "Don't jump to conclusions," he added, as if he could hear what she was thinking. "The situation is just a little more complicated than I was told, which means I'm stuck here for the weekend."

"Are you having a good time?" She didn't want to sound like a nag, so she attempted to be cheerful.

"I don't know if you could call it a good time," Jake answered slowly. "I've had to sit through a few long meetings. The show's ratings have dropped. They want to bring me back from the dead as my twin brother for a few episodes, and then kill me all over again."

"Can they do that?"

"Sure. They're writers," Jake said, as if that explained everything.

"Oh." Leah decided it was time to change the topic of conversation. She didn't want Jake to know how badly she missed him. *Keep it light, Leah.* "The confirmation for the Vermont house came in the mail today. It looks wonderful. There's a colored picture of the place surrounded by snow and mountains. Do you still want to go?"

"Don't you?"

"Well..." She hesitated, not wanting him to hear the disappointment in her voice. After all, he hadn't given her a direct answer. "It's—"

"Leah, hon, I have to go now." His voice grew stronger, and Leah realized he probably hadn't even been listening to her.

"Okay."

"See you soon." He was gone.

"Bye." She hung up the phone softly. The kitchen was dark and gloomy in the late afternoon.

Her eyes burned, so she closed them for a moment. Not with tears. Her eyes were tired from reading, and she still had to start typing the final draft of the big psych paper. She'd been studying for two tests, one in history and another in American poets.

Screw American poets.

Maybe he's not coming back. A nasty truth, but still, it hung in the air like impending doom. Jake could pretend to be his twin brother and make a lot more money, living in Hollywood with his fancy friends. There he'd never have to hammer another nail, take a six-year-old out for pizza, carve pumpkins or share a turkey dinner with people who had never even been mentioned in *TV Guide*....

I'm feeling sorry for myself again. Leah went back into the living room to face the textbooks stacked on her desk. This self-pity routine wasn't going to get any work done. She concentrated on the books for an hour until Julia dropped off Willie.

"Uh-oh," Julia said, looking at the papers and books strewn around the living room and spilling from the desk. "It looks like your brain exploded. That time of the semester, huh?"

"Yep. Want coffee? I'm overdue for a fresh pot of caffeine."

Julia looked at her watch. "Well, okay, if you're sure I'm not disturbing you."

"You're not. I'm just sitting here feeling sorry for myself. Must be the holiday blues."

Julia followed her into the kitchen. "How are you doing with your Christmas shopping?"

"I haven't done much more," Leah answered, going to the sink to fill the glass carafe. "I'll have to wait until after the seventeenth, when I have time to think."

"Still planning on Christmas in Vermont with Jake? I envy you."

"Don't. Jake's not around right now." She quickly finished filling the coffeepot and turned on the switch. "There. That won't take long."

"It's just a business trip," Julia reminded her. She sat down at the kitchen table and tugged off her heavy coat.

Leah joined her. "Maybe. Maybe not."

"I go nuts when Harry leaves for more than two days. At first it's nice to give the kids toasted cheese sandwiches for dinner, but after a while the nights get really long."

Leah remembered the nights all too well. "I know."

"How serious is it between you two, Leah?"

"We haven't talked too much about the future, if that's what you mean. He told me we'd go to Bermuda when I graduated, but he might have been teasing."

"That's years from now. I think that qualifies as talking about the future, don't you?"

Leah shrugged. "Maybe I'm not ready to think about the future, except for getting my degree. Everything else has to wait."

"You love him."

"Sure."

"You've told him, he's told you?"

Leah nodded. "Yes."

Julia breathed a sigh that sounded like relief. "I was afraid you'd keep your feelings inside on that one."

"Why?"

"You're a very private person, Leah. We've been friends for a long time, and yet..."

"Yet?" Leah prodded.

"I've never seen you...show a lot of emotion about things," Julia told her.

Leah rested her chin in her hands, considering her friend's comment. "Another one of my problems?"

Julia smiled. "Possibly. You're a pretty self-contained unit."

"True," Leah agreed. "I haven't had much choice."

"Now you do."

"Maybe," she said, standing up to pour coffee. "Maybe not. I guess I'll just have to wait and see."

LEAH TRIED to navigate the grocery cart through the mob of shoppers. It seemed as if everyone in southern Rhode Island was stocking up for the holidays, and it was only December 9. The holiday season was clearly in full swing. Leah struggled to manage a very long grocery list, a worn envelope filled with coupons, and a rambunctious Willie, who was trying to push the cart towards the candy aisle whenever his mother wasn't looking. Canned Christmas music blared in the background, testing Leah's holiday spirit.

She gave up. Two-thirds of the way through the gigantic store, Leah grabbed whatever items she thought she needed without regard to coupons or consulting her neatly typed list. She finished the last four aisles in record time, then pushed her overflowing cart into the long line at the checkout.

Leah stepped over to the magazines to browse through

the Christmas issues. After all, there wasn't anything else to do while she stood in line with half the adult population of Narragansett. She read the headlines in *Cosmopolitan*, looking for anything of interest. *Good Housekeeping*'s annual cover with the elaborate gingerbread house looked gorgeous, but didn't tempt her to purchase the magazine to help her attempt to construct her own.

Out of simple curiosity she looked at the gossip magazines. Leah had to read the words twice before they sank in. The harsh, black print on the magazine cover read Jeffrey Kent Father at Last?

Father?

Leah stepped closer. A grainy photograph showed Jake and Sybil Cole arm in arm. Sybil wore a full, waistless dress—no one would be able to guess whether or not she was pregnant, but it was an uncharacteristic outfit for the slinky Sybil to wear. Jake looked angry, an unusual grimace on his handsome face. Leah pulled the copy of *True Gossip* out of its holder above the conveyor belt and scanned the brief caption under the photo. "Out of hiding, Jason Masters confronts Sybil's accusations. What's next for the stars of *Fascination* and their dynamite new relationship? Continued on page 21."

The checkout line moved forward. The woman in front of Leah pulled a case of disposable diapers and two twelve-packs of diet cola from her cart, while Leah tried to locate page 21.

"Sybil Cole, sexy star of television's *Fascination*, seems to be fascinated with her former costar in many ways. 'I've missed him dreadfully—'"

"Mom," Willie interrupted. "Your turn."

"Oh." She closed the paper, but didn't want to put it down. She tucked it under her arm and reached into her cart to start loading the groceries onto the belt. "William," she ordered firmly, "start piling the food up here."

He did, and Leah quickly thumbed to page 21 to read the rest. "'I've missed him dreadfully,' she said, 'in more ways than one.' And where was Jeffrey when Sybil needed him? The sexy and vibrant Miss Cole has secrets of her own these days, and one of them—"

"Ma'am?"

She looked up at the checkout boy, a young man about college age. "Yes?"

"Are you ready?"

Leah realized that she needed to keep unloading her cart. "Oh. Sorry." She felt her face grow warm; she'd been holding up the line because she was engrossed in the latest edition of *True Gossip*. Leah tossed the paper onto the belt and bent over to scoop cans of soup from the bottom of the cart, as Willie sneaked a candy bar between three boxes of cereal and a head of lettuce. Leah let him. He could have candy bars for dinner, if he'd leave her alone while she finished reading the article in the paper.

She remembered the coupons in time, wrote a check, and handed the young man her identification card with thinly disguised impatience.

Father at last.

Leah finished packing the groceries into paper bags with the assistance of a teenage girl. Trying to hurry, she tossed the soup on top of the lettuce. She didn't care if the fabric softener sheets were packed with the bag of apples, or that the cans of frozen orange juice weren't wrapped in plastic bags. She didn't care if her flour smelled of garlic. She wanted to get out of the store and into the car, where she could read about Jake's sex life in relative peace.

"I'll take that," Leah said, pulling the *True Gossip* from the girl's hands. She shoved it inside her purse.

"You said that was junk," Willie observed, eyeing the paper his mother had just tucked into her bag.

"It is. I like junk."

The teenager piled the final bag onto the cart. "Have a nice day."

It was a little late to have a nice day, Leah thought, but she smiled politely. "Come on." She grabbed Willie. "Zip up your coat and put your hat on."

"Mom," he wailed as the automatic doors opened. "I don't know where she put the candy bar."

"You'll find it." Wind whipped around the parking lot, and Leah forced the cart through the flurries of snow to the car. After she unlocked it and told Willie to climb in, Leah piled grocery bags around him, then got behind the wheel and shut the door.

"You're supposed to return the cart to the store," he said.

"I know. I will in a minute."

Leah flipped the page back to where she'd been reading, while her son rustled through the bags.

"I thought you said those papers were all silly."

"They are. I feel like reading something silly, all right?"

"Why?"

She didn't want him to see Jake's name or picture. "For school," was the first thing she could think of. "It's homework."

He seemed satisfied with that, and rummaged through the bags until he found the missing chocolate.

Leah read. The article was ambiguous, of course. It didn't actually state that Jake was the father of Sybil's baby, and didn't exactly quote Sybil about her pregnancy. Just "sources next to the famous and lovely superstar" hinted at possible motherhood.

"Where there's smoke, there's fire," her grandmother would have said. Leah tossed the paper onto the seat and grabbed the keys out of her coat pocket. Fat, white snow-flakes turned to slush as they hit the windshield, and Leah shivered as she watched them.

"I hafta go to the bathroom."

Leah didn't know how long she would have sat there, watching snowflakes splatter against the glass. "Me, too," she answered, and put the key into the ignition. She hopped out of the car and guiltily pushed the cart into a group with other carts. She felt like throwing up.

The phone was ringing as they entered the house. Willie rushed around the corner to the bathroom, and Leah ignored the phone's shrill demands. Did any of her friends read *True Gossip*? She doubted it. She would have to call Julia and Pat and try to figure this out. The ringing stopped as Leah placed an armload of damp, brown bags on the kitchen table. She took a deep breath, walked over to the telephone and unplugged it from its socket. She laid it gently on the counter and went back outside for another load of groceries.

The snowflakes had turned into fat pellets of water. December 9, Leah grumbled to herself, and there hadn't been even the skimpiest layer of snow to enjoy.

Snow reminded her of Vermont and Christmas, so she tried to think of something else as she trudged back and forth from the car to the house in the miserable night. Her feet, even encased in her thickest boots, were cold, and her hair hung in wet lanks from her ivory knit cap. Leah tried to think of today's class and the work involved in finishing up the project by next week.

Much later, after the food had been put away, when she'd heated up chicken nuggets and French fries for dinner and had tucked her child into bed after he'd read her part of a story, Leah took a shower and put on her longest, oldest, ugliest flannel nightgown and began to feel better.

"I love your nightgowns," Jake had said.

Leah looked down at the faded flannel. He wouldn't love this one, she thought with satisfaction. She took *True Gossip* from its hiding place on top of the refrigerator and plugged in the phone once again.

She could handle things now, and who would call at nine-thirty to tell her that her boyfriend had made the cover of a supermarket tabloid?

Five minutes later the phone rang. She picked it up with little enthusiasm. "Hello?"

"Leah?" Jake's voice was concerned. "Are you okay? I've been calling for hours."

"I was doing errands," she lied. "Grocery shopping."

"Look, hon, there's something I need to talk to you about."

"Father at Last?" she asked.

"You saw it?"

"It's sitting on the kitchen table right now. I bought eighty-eight dollars' worth of food and spent an extra seventy-five cents to read about your sex life."

"It's all lies," he said quietly.

What else had she expected him to say? "You're not the father of Sybil's baby?"

"Of course not. I've never even slept with her, except in front of the cameras."

"How can they just print lies like this, then?"

"I haven't seen the article, Leah, but chances are they were careful to dance around the facts."

"I think you'd better buy a copy."

"I wouldn't waste the money."

"When are you coming back, Jake?"

He sighed. Leah could picture him frowning absently into space. "I'm not sure."

"Okay." She wondered how long it would take her to get over him. "No problem."

"Don't take the newspaper too seriously, hon. This sort of thing happens all the time and it doesn't mean anything."

It does to me. "By 'that sort of thing' do you mean sex, pregnancy or articles in the paper?"

"It's a publicity stunt," he insisted. "That's all."

"Good night, Jake."

"I love you, hon."

Leah didn't answer. She replaced the receiver, wondering how she could have fallen in love with a phony actor who had deserted a pregnant woman and hidden in a church.

"I CAN'T WAIT. How many more days?"

"Till Christmas?"

"Yeah," Willie pleaded. "How many more days?"

Leah looked at the calendar inside the kitchen cupboard. "Not counting today, eleven."

"Jeez," he complained. Then his face brightened. "How many days till we go away?"

She sighed, hating to lie to him. "I don't know, Willie."

"We're going, aren't we?"

Could they go to Vermont by themselves? The Subaru wouldn't have any trouble making it. Front-wheel drive was supposed to zip right along through snow. She could get a map of New England or follow the directions on the brochure. But to go without Jake? "I don't know yet," she replied honestly.

"When's Jake coming home?"

"I don't know that, either. The last time I talked to him on the phone, he said he didn't know how long he had to stay." That was three days ago. She longed to hear his voice, but he hadn't called.

"I hope it's gonna be soon." Willie sighed with all the vehemence a disappointed boy could muster. "Nobody knows nuthin' around here." He grabbed a cookie from the bag on the table and stood up.

"Eat it over the table," she said automatically. Store bought Christmas cookies. Her grandmother was probably turning over in her grave.

"I hope Santa brings me a squirt gun."

"You might land in jail. Don't get any ideas. I've had enough trouble teaching you not to trespass."

"Yeah."

"But we have that all straightened out," she insisted. "Right?"

"No problem." He grinned at her.

The answer sounded so much like Jake. Leah hadn't realized how much her son copied his hero's expressions.

"Don't ruin your dinner," she insisted crossly. She was swamped, overtired, lonely, miserable and crabby; she wanted the semester to end and Jake to come home, so that life could turn into one, long, Christmas holiday. She wanted to sing "White Christmas" with Bing Crosby on the radio and really mean the words. Leah decided she desperately needed some Christmas spirit.

AT FIRST she didn't hear the knock on the door. When she opened it, she found Julia and Pat waiting patiently in the dark.

"You need some Christmas spirit," Patsy said.

"And hot crab dip." Julia held a covered casserole with mittened hands. A box of wheat crackers rested on top of the tinfoil.

Pat waved a bottle. "Wine. We decided it's been an awful

week and since it's Friday, we had to get away from our families for a while. I think we all need a break."

"This is a great idea, but I have papers due in three days."

"We won't stay long," Pat cajoled, as the two friends entered the house. "It's only five o'clock. I don't work on Fridays, so Julia and I have been Christmas shopping."

Leah was ridiculously relieved to have company. "How did you know I was sinking into depression?"

"You wouldn't talk on the phone," Julia said. "That indicates real stress."

"We've both been grocery shopping this week," Patsy added. "We've seen the headlines."

"Father at Last?" Leah asked, wincing.

Julia nodded and stepped into the kitchen. The others followed. "Jake doesn't seem like the love 'em and leave 'em type."

Leah frowned. "He is on television."

"That's different," Julia argued. "He's a good actor, so it's easy to believe he'd be like that in real life."

"I didn't see a red truck in the driveway," Pat said. "Is the star still in California?"

Leah nodded, reaching into the cupboard for glasses. "I talked to him on Monday. He said the whole thing with Sybil was all a lie."

"Of course it is. Have some dip." Julia peeled the tinfoil from the top of the dish. "I'll dump these crackers in a dish."

"I'll open the bottle."

Leah suspected her friends felt sorry for her. Here she'd finally met a wonderful man, and he turned out to be more than anyone had bargained for. She was glad to change the subject. "Remember when we used to have those Christmas cookie exchanges, and ten of us would bake and then get together with the kids all crawling around, while we exchanged ten different kinds of cookies?"

Pat winced. "I'd shoot myself if I had to do that this year. Drinking champagne and eating crab dip are much more civilized." She popped the cork and spilled the foamy liquid into three crystal glasses.

"Amen," Julia said.

Willie looked into the kitchen. "Hi! You guys having a party?"

"Yes," Leah answered. "You can watch TV or play in your room."

"When's dinner?" he asked suspiciously.

"Later."

"Much later. Let's toast to Christmas spirit," Pat suggested. "May we all survive the next eleven days."

ELEVEN DAYS. It didn't feel like Christmas, Jake thought, looking out of the sliding glass door onto the deck that faced Malibu beach. A friend—skiing in Switzerland—had loaned him the house. Staying here gave him an odd feeling of permanency, much more than he'd have had in a hotel.

He thought he might have liked the hotel better. At least there'd have been people and restaurants and a bar only an elevator ride away.

Jake looked out at the Pacific Ocean with little enthusiasm. Eleven days until Christmas, and he was on the West Coast with no evergreens, no snow and no Leah. A dozen parties, though, could occupy his weekend—if he wanted them to.

And a new episode of *Fascination* went into rehearsal, first thing Monday morning. Jake walked away from the stunning Malibu sunset and reached for the telephone.

"Leah," he said, when he heard her voice.

"Jake?"

"Hi, hon." He brushed his copy of the script aside and sank into the white couch. "How are you?"

"I'm good." Her voice sounded sleepy.

"Did I wake you up?"

"Oh, no. It's after ten, but I've been studying. Everything is due next week, so this weekend has to count."

"How's it going?" He worried about her.

"I'll make it."

"How's Will?"

"Waiting for Christmas."

"Me, too." The silence filled the phone line. Jake struggled to think of what to say. He wanted her to keep talking so he could continue to hear her voice. The words weren't important. "How's your Abnormal Behavior class?"

"Intense. I'll finish the paper this weekend and have the final on Tuesday. How has your week been?"

"Fine. Busy. I didn't call because I knew you were occupied with school and studying. I didn't want to disturb you."

"Thanks," she said softly. "It's been really busy here, too."

"Have you been over to the church?"

"No, but I saw a painter's van parked in the lot."

"Good. I put one of the guys in charge of keeping things going."

The silence stretched between them. "I'd better go."

"All right. I'll call you next week."

"Bye, Jake."

"Bye, hon." Jake wanted to tell her he'd be back in Rhode Island soon, wanted to assure her that his plans for Christmas hadn't changed, but the words stuck in his throat. He'd promised himself he would never lie to her again.

"MRS. LANG?"

Leah was on her way out the door to Monday morning's history lecture when she stopped to answer the phone. "Yes. Speaking."

"This is Bob Petty from Seaside Properties in Wakefield. Jake Kennedy said you had an extra key to the Pritchard's Corner Baptist Church."

Leah didn't know what the man was talking about. "I'm sorry," she said slowly, "but I don't understand."

The man's voice was easy, friendly and unruffled. "He said he left an extra set in the house he rents from you in Pritchard's Corner. Would it be all right if I stopped by this morning to pick them up?"

"He didn't mention it to me." What did this mean? she worried.

"I just talked to him this morning," he said. "I'm sure he'll be calling you about it."

"All right, then." She glanced at her watch. "I'm leaving now, but if I can find the keys, I'll leave them in the mailbox for you."

"He said they're hanging on a hook by the sink."

She knew the man must have talked to Jake. "Okay. The mailbox says Lang and is # 2382."

"Thank you very much."

"You're welcome."

Leah hung up the phone and automatically picked up her heavy winter coat. With a feeling of dread she trudged through the cold, the smell of wood burning in a neighbor's stove filling her nostrils and making her long for a fireplace like the one her grandmother had had in the farmhouse.

The plumber's truck was parked in front. The weekend had been a nightmare. The farmhouse's septic tank had overflowed, leaving six girls no way to get ready for a special holiday party. Leah didn't know if she'd spent more time studying or cleaning yesterday. How could she be worn out, when the week hadn't even started yet?

She fumbled through the keys on the ring until she found the one to unlock Jake's door. The cottage was warm, so she turned the heat down to save money. The clump of keys was where the real-estate agent had said it would be, so Leah stuck it into her pocket and left.

It was time she faced facts. Jake had left for California, had not said when he was coming back, and now was giving a real-estate agent the keys to the church. His name had been linked with another woman, who claimed she was having his baby. Maybe he'd discovered he was the father, after all.

Maybe he had to sell the church to pay her off.

No more maybes. Leah trudged to her car.

The guy wasn't coming back.

12

PATSY CLEARED HER THROAT. "There must be a perfectly reasonable explanation."

"I don't think I can come up with one right this minute," Leah said. She'd stopped the car in the middle of Old Post Road when she'd seen the For Sale sign, stuck in the small patch of lawn in front of the church. "A real-estate agent picked up the keys this morning. He certainly didn't waste any time."

"Don't jump to any conclusions until you've talked to Jake," Pat warned. "Okay?"

"Well," she answered grimly, stepping on the gas. "Look on the bright side—at least I don't have to worry anymore about what to buy him for Christmas." Leah drove down the street to Patsy's house and dropped off her friend at the bottom of her driveway.

"Thanks again for the ride home. Are you sure you don't want to come in for coffee?"

"Thanks, but Willie will be home soon, and I still have to cram for a final tomorrow."

"Well, good luck. Call if you need someone to talk to, okay?"

"I'll be fine." Leah turned the car around and headed back home. She needed a lot more than luck to mend a broken heart. Even studying for finals and cleaning up the mess at the farmhouse hadn't kept her thoughts from Jake, from trying to put the pieces together into some sort of pattern. Jake had said he was never going back to L.A., but he had gone back there. He'd said he didn't want to act anymore, yet he'd returned to *Fascination* and stardom. He'd denied ever having an affair with Sybil Cole, though the newspapers accused him of being the father of her baby. He'd bought the church, but the For Sale sign told her that Jake had abandoned Pritchard's Corner and wasn't coming back.

Exhausted, she parked the car and went into the house. The place was a real pit, she hadn't cooked a real meal in a week, and there were still Christmas presents to buy, but at least she'd survived the first semester.

Leah was mentally creating a new list of things to do when the school bus deposited Willie in front of the house. He ran into the kitchen, his brown eyes brimming with tears. "Mom! Why is Jake's church on sale?"

"Honey," she soothed, crouching in front of him so that they were on the same level. "I really don't know. Maybe Jake is so busy in California that he can't come back."

Willie sniffed. "He's comin' back. He promised."

How could she explain to a little boy that promises got broken, and that even the best-looking heroes could turn out to be mere mortals, who hurt other people when they changed their minds? "Well, we'll see."

Much later that evening, as Leah sat hunched over her desk in the living room, she listened to her son inconsolably cry himself to sleep.

"WHY DID the chicken cross the road?"

Leah cradled the receiver against her ear while she spread red frosting on top of a cupcake. "I give up, Paul. Why?"

"To eat the seed out of our bird feeder."

"Oh, no. Alien must be loose again. I'll send Willie over to chase her home."

"That's okay. I think she's gone now."

"Tell your folks I'm sorry. I'll buy you a new bag of seed the next time I'm in town." She counted the cupcakes lined up on the counter. Twenty-four should be enough for the first-grade Christmas party tomorrow.

"My mom thought it was pretty funny. Thanks for typing my English Lit paper— I got a B."

"Well, thanks for helping me out Tuesday. I appreciated your babysitting on a school night." The impromptu gathering at Julia's to celebrate Patsy's birthday had coincided with her last day of exams. It had been so much fun to relax for a change.

"No problem. Have a good time in Vermont, and Merry Christmas!"

"You, too, Paul," Leah said, hanging up the phone. Vermont? She hadn't yet decided whether to go. Willie must be telling stories again. She put the knife into the sink and went over to the refrigerator. A ladybug magnet held a skiing brochure to the shiny metal door, and the confirmation of the chalet rental was tucked safely inside Leah's desk drawer.

Everything was paid for. It was all Willie wanted for Christmas; he'd cheered up considerably in the last couple of days and talked about nothing else but learning how to ski.

Why shouldn't she go? Leah tucked the cupcakes into a plastic container and set them on the table, so they wouldn't be forgotten. She needed a vacation. It would be her first holiday since she was twelve years old. She would be away from her computer, away from her textbooks, away from the worry of what grades she received in her courses, and alone with her little boy. If she was going to keep up the pace for many more years of college, she needed to give herself a break.

"TIME TO GET IN THE CAR!" Leah tried for what she hoped was a cheerful-mother tone. Willie was so excited that she felt guilty for even considering not going. Pulling out of the empty driveway gave her a positive sensation. The girls had gone to their respective homes for the vacation. With both them and Jake gone, the parking area was bare and silent.

It turned out to be a miserable drive. The traffic wasn't bad for a Saturday morning, but the Subaru's windshield wipers slogged rhythmically through the rain for several hours, until Leah drove out of Massachusetts and into Vermont along Interstate 91.

Sugarbush Valley wasn't too difficult to find, although Leah felt as if she'd driven through most of Vermont before finding the town of Warren and the nearby ski area. She stopped at the real-estate office for the keys and directions to the chalet, let Willie use the bathroom, then headed up into the mountains before dark. A dead-end, twisting road finally led her to a gorgeous house that seemed to cling to the sides of the snow-covered mountain. Huge, glass doors faced a massive deck piled high with snow.

So this was Jake's Christmas present to her. She tried not to think about him as she followed the road to the back of the big house and parked in front of a garage.

"Wow! This is neat!"

"Do you really think this is the place?" Why was she asking a six-year-old for an opinion?

"Come on, Mom, let's go!" Willie hopped out of the car and bounded through the snow like an eager puppy.

Leah took her time tromping through the snow. She fumbled with the keys until she found the one that unlocked the back door, then cautiously pushed it open. Willie flipped all the switches on the wall, and the foyer was suddenly filled with light. Empty ski racks formed part of the doorless closet to her left, and smooth, beige carpet caught the snow they'd tracked in.

"Take off your boots," she said automatically, bending over to tug off her own.

They stepped into the enormous kitchen-dining-living-room area, which soared to a cathedral ceiling. Ivory walls, beige carpet and the neutral tones of the simple furniture combined for a feeling of elegance and comfort. Off to one side stood a massive, stone fireplace, and in front of them was a wall of thick drapes. Leah hurried to open them. When she did, the breathtaking view of snow-covered mountains entranced her. She figured she could have stood there until dark, but Willie raced up the stairs.

"Come on, Mom!" She followed him. An assortment of beds and couches filled the vast loft. "Can I sleep up here? Please?"

"Sure. If you want." She left him upstairs and explored downstairs. A master bedroom, complete with king-size bed, Jacuzzi and tiled bath, lay beyond the living room. It also had a breathtaking view and, Leah decided, was bigger than her entire house. She discovered two smaller bedrooms and another bathroom before returning to the kitchen to poke around in the cupboards.

Everything was immaculate. The dishes matched. The built-in dishwasher was another touch of heaven. It was the perfect place, Leah reflected, to nurse a broken heart and forget that Jake Kennedy had ever waltzed into Rhode Island.

"HE'S COMING. I know he is."

Leah turned away from the glass doors and the view of

the mountains to look at her son. He sat defiantly on the couch, an unfinished jigsaw puzzle on the table in front of him. Yesterday they'd found two shelves of puzzles in the hall closet, and now Leah knew why: no television, not another living creature in sight, and the snow continued to fall. The ski area was several miles away, and Leah had discovered their skiing lessons at Sugarbush Valley weren't scheduled until the day after Christmas. And to top it all off, today was Christmas Eve.

"He's working in California. You know that."

"Nobody works on Christmas, 'cept Santa."

He's a fake, too. But her son's irrefutable logic left her with nothing to say. She'd raised him to believe in fairy tales and this was her punishment. What else did she expect? "Want to go to town to see a movie?"

"Nah."

"Want to go sledding again?" Their inspection of the garage had yielded several old wooden sleds, a sleek toboggan and a couple of plastic saucers.

"Nah."

"Want hot chocolate? We could turn off the lights and plug in the tree."

"It's afternoon."

"We'll close the curtains."

"Okay."

Leah plugged the cord into the outlet behind the tree, while Willie closed the drapes. It wasn't a real tree. They'd very conveniently found an artificial one in the garage, too, boxed up and ready to be assembled. Leah had done some fast talking to convince her son that cutting down one of the trees in the back yard would be illegal. She'd hauled all their ornaments and lights from Pritchard's Corner; the artificial tree was the answer to her prayers. Of course, she thought wearily, decorating had only taken an hour. One hour out of two and a half days.

The different colors blinked in the murky light, while Leah heated water in the teakettle and Willie dumped packets of instant hot chocolate into mugs. "Wanna play Monopoly?"

"Sure." Leah poured the hot water into the cups and let Willie stir, then popped a tape of Christmas songs into the expensive stereo system that was built into the wall. This would be a Christmas she would never forget—for all the wrong reasons. She took a deep breath and willed away the tears before returning to the kitchen. "Want some more cookies?"

Playing the simplified version of Monopoly, geared to a six-year-old's understanding, the thrill of spending play money wore off after a couple of hours. But Leah had another plan to keep Willie occupied. Having determinedly saved the carefully arranged logs in the stone fireplace for Christmas Eve, she touched matches to the paper now and kept her fingers crossed that whoever prepared the wood had known what he or she was doing. The flames caught, and soon the wood burned merrily, crackling and popping, sounding positively homey.

They roasted hot dogs on skewers over the flames, eating the crispy result while sitting on the hearth, then sang Christmas songs while the tree lights blinked on and off in bright patterns.

"I know he'll be here," Willie declared, swallowing the head of a gingerbread-man cookie.

"Santa?"

"Jake."

"Honey, you can't go on believing that."

"He promised."

"Promises get broken," Leah tried to tell him gently. "Even though people have the best intentions."

"He's gonna come," Willie insisted. He wrapped his arms around Leah's neck and hugged her tightly. "You gotta believe me."

She clung to him, wishing she knew what to say. "Okay," she finally answered. "I'll try."

After that he sat patiently in front of the cold expanse of glass, staring into the night. It broke her heart to see him sit there, watching and waiting. "Remember last year?" she asked. "You looked out of your bedroom window, waiting to see Rudolph's red nose up in the sky."

"Yeah." He grinned at her. "I saw it, too."

"Have you seen any flashing red lights tonight?"

Willie shook his head. "Not yet."

He wasn't watching for Rudolph, she knew. He never took his gaze from the dark road.

Another hour crawled by. Leah assembled two animals from the elaborate jungle puzzle before looking at her watch. Eight-thirty. "Bedtime," she announced, straightening her stiff back. Several attempts later, she managed to get his attention. He left milk and cookies for Santa on the dining-room table before letting her tuck him into his bed in the loft. Willie kissed her eight times and made her promise to go to bed early, so Santa Claus could come.

"Go to sleep," Leah told her son with a chuckle.

"Tell Jake I had t'go t'bed."

"I will," she fibbed, and went downstairs to the empty living room. She killed more time by clearing the food away, putting the few dirty dishes into the dishwasher and wiping off the kitchen's long stretch of butcher-block countertop. Then she plopped onto the couch and listened to the silence as she looked at the perfectly symmetrical tree. Great. A fake tree. Someone else's house. Not another person in sight. *Merry Christmas to me.* In a few years, looking back on this particular holiday, the pain would not be so strong, but right now the night remained bleak.

Cheer up, she told herself. It couldn't be as bad as staying at home.

Leah got up, fixed herself a cup of tea and went back to the puzzle. She found all of the pieces of the elephant, then slipped on her boots and jacket to unload the presents from Santa that were still hidden in the trunk of the car.

Leah decided she'd have to make a couple of trips. Most of the tissue-wrapped gifts were contained in heavy shopping bags, but the wrestling ring was too big. She struggled with the bulky packages until one fell into the snow.

"Damn." She reached for it, the wet, green tissue staining her fingers as she picked up the package.

"Ho, ho, ho," a deep voice said behind her.

Leah froze, her heart in her throat.

"What do *you* want for Christmas, Ms. Lang?"

There was no mistaking the voice. Leah wheeled around, the packages still in her arms. Jake stood four feet away, a red knit cap on his head, his down vest over the familiar, red flannel shirt, and a bag slung over his shoulder. "What in hell are you doing here?"

Jake grinned. "Is that a nice way to greet Santa, young lady?" His breath came out in little puffs as he laughed.

"This isn't funny. You could have given me a heart attack." She looked past his shoulders to the road, but there was no car. "How did you get up here?"

"My rental car couldn't make it up the last hill. I had to throw what I could in my bag and hike the rest of the way. I'm sorry I'm late. All the flights were stacked up over New York. I am so damn glad to see you...." He set his bag down in the snow and stepped forward, as if to take her in his arms.

"Stop right there," she ordered. "I want to know what you think you're doing."

He looked surprised. "Having Christmas with you and the kid, just like we planned."

Leah felt like committing murder. "Just like we *planned*?"

"Whoa! What am I supposed to have done wrong?"

"Wrong?" she echoed. "You're supposed to be the father of Sybil Cole's baby, you're back on *Fascination*—and you're selling the church."

"Where are you getting these ideas?" Jake sighed, running his hand through his snow-dusted hair. "Sybil isn't pregnant—it was a publicity stunt, just as I told you a couple of weeks ago. I'm not staying in L.A. I just did it for the money, and—" he winked cheerfully at her "—I made a ton of it."

"Good for you."

"Good for us."

"Us?"

"I didn't go out there for the fun of it. I did it for us—now there's money for your schooling, and you won't have to work or be a landlady or type papers."

"I can?"

"Sure. I thought it would help you, not make you mad. If we're careful about investing the rest, Willie's education will be all set, too. And any other kids we might have."

"Other kids?" Leah felt disoriented.

"Sure." Jake stepped even closer and looked down at her, his charcoal eyes filled with tenderness. "Haven't you tried to teach me to plan ahead?" He held out his hands. "Let me take these packages."

Leah numbly let him remove the bags from her stiff arms as she tried to absorb his words. He acted as if he'd been away on business—nothing more, nothing less. "What about the church?"

"The real-estate agent jumped the gun on that one." He nodded toward the door. "Could we talk about this inside?"

"Uh-uh."

Jake frowned. "You thought I wasn't coming back."

She didn't have to say anything. He looked as if he was going to dump the packages into the snow and stomp off down the mountainside.

"You automatically assumed—in that damn independent, idiotic way of yours—that I'd lied and cheated and wasn't coming back. Thanks a lot."

"But," she offered weakly, "the For Sale sign..."

"I intended to talk to you about it, but I also tried to leave you alone, so you could study. You didn't need nightly calls from me on top of everything else last week. I wanted to use the profits from the church to renovate your old farmhouse. I thought you'd rather have that place as your home than the church." He glared at her. "Was I right?"

"Yes." Jake was very, very right.

"There's something called trust, lady. It's okay to need people. It's okay to learn to trust the person who loves you."

"And I flunked," she said softly.

"Damn right you did."

"I didn't know you were coming back."

"Willie was supposed to tell you I was coming. I talked to him on the phone Tuesday night, when you were out. Didn't he?"

He's coming. I know he is. You gotta believe me. "I didn't believe him."

Jake's tight expression relaxed. "I can't imagine why not."

"I think he's learned his lesson."

"What about you?"

I've learned I'm an idiotic fool who doesn't know a good thing when she has it. "The way I see it, we have three choices," she managed. Jake waited, his arms still full of bulky presents. "You can stomp off into the night, refusing to accept my heartfelt apologies."

Jake stepped beside her and dumped the gifts back into the trunk. Leah's stomach dropped. Was he angry enough with her to actually leave?

"Or?"

"Or we can be friends."

He put his large, gloved hands onto her shoulders and looked down at her, his expression unreadable. "Or?"

Good. He wanted to hear her third option. "Or," she said, her voice soft as she looked up into his gorgeous, familiar face, "we can go inside the house, Santa, put the presents under the tree and make love until morning."

Jake shook his head, and Leah turned cold. "Not just until morning, Leah, but for the rest of our lives."

Leah nodded, relief and happiness singing through her like a chorus of angels. He kissed her for a long moment, warming her cold lips as she clung to him, gripping the flannel sleeves of his shirt to hold him to her until they both gasped for air.

"Jake, wait—"

"What now?" His eyes darkened.

Embarrassment and guilt filled her. "I didn't get you a Christmas present."

Jake bundled her into his arms and she felt his chest shake with laughter. "Sweetheart, will you ever understand that I already have everything I could ever want?"

EARLY THE NEXT MORNING, Jake peered through the murky light of dawn to see a small figure tiptoe up to the bed and peer at the sleeping Leah, without realizing there was an-other person beside her.

"Hey, kid!" Jake whispered. Willie's face lit up as he scrambled over Leah to embrace his hero. A strong feeling of contentment washed over Jake as he held the boy in his arms.

"You're back!" Willie whispered.

"Yeah," Jake said gruffly.

"You gonna stay?"

Jake nodded. "For a long, long time."

Willie thought that over for a second. "Santa Claus came last night."

"He did?"

"Wanna see?"

"Sure." Jake sat up. "Hand me my pants, will you?"

"Okay." Willie hopped out of the bed, found the pants on the floor and shoved them across the blankets. "Mom didn't think you were gonna come, but I knew you would."

"I know. She told me."

"She doesn't believe in *anything*." Willie hesitated. "'Cept Santa."

"Not true," Leah mumbled sleepily. She struggled to sit up, but her flowered-print nightgown caught in the blan-kets. Jake reached over and helped untangle her. "I believe in lots of things," she said, smiling at the two people she loved more than anything else in the world. "I believe in happy endings. Is that good enough?"

"It's good enough for me." Jake caressed her cheek with a gentle fingertip.

"You know," Willie added thoughtfully, tugging on Jake's arm to force him out of bed. "I like you, even if you're not Superman."

"Me, too," Leah said, looking at the man she trusted with all her heart. "Me, too."

LOOK FOR OUR FOUR FABULOUS MEN!

Each month some of today's bestselling authors bring
four new fabulous men to Harlequin American Romance.
Whether they're rebel ranchers, millionaire power brokers
or sexy single dads, they're all gallant princes—and
they're all ready to sweep you into lighthearted fantasies
and contemporary fairy tales where anything is possible
and where all your dreams come true!

You don't even have to make a wish...
Harlequin American Romance will grant your every desire!

Look for Harlequin American Romance
wherever Harlequin books are sold!

HARLEQUIN PRESENTS®

HARLEQUIN PRESENTS
men you won't be able to resist
falling in love with...

HARLEQUIN PRESENTS
women who have feelings
just like your own...

HARLEQUIN PRESENTS
powerful passion in
exotic international settings...

HARLEQUIN PRESENTS
intense, dramatic stories that will keep you
turning to the very last page...

HARLEQUIN PRESENTS
The world's bestselling romance series!

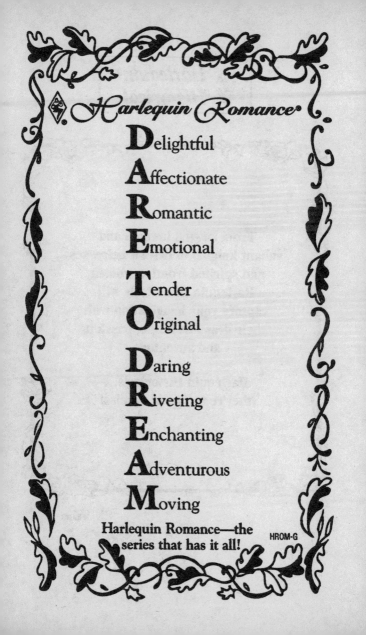

Harlequin Romance®

Delightful

Affectionate

Romantic

Emotional

Tender

Original

Daring

Riveting

Enchanting

Adventurous

Moving

Harlequin Romance—the
series that has it all!

HROM-G

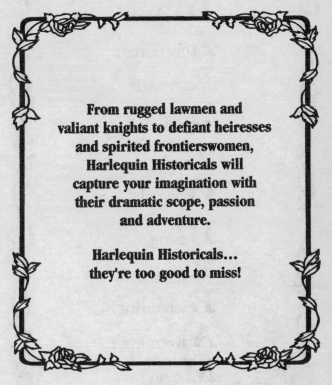

HHGENR

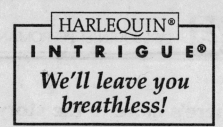

HARLEQUIN SUPERROMANCE®

...there's more to the story!

Superromance. A *big* satisfying read about unforgettable characters. Each month we offer *four* very different stories that range from family drama to adventure and mystery, from highly emotional stories to romantic comedies—and much more! Stories about people you'll believe in and care about. Stories too compelling to put down....

Our authors are among today's *best* romance writers. You'll find familiar names and talented newcomers. Many of them are award winners—and you'll see why!

If you want the biggest and best in romance fiction, you'll get it from Superromance!

Available wherever Harlequin books are sold.